THE END OF TIME

BOOK 3 IN THE CASTLETON SERIES

By Mike Dunbar

a division of Soul Star Multimedia, LLC

1621 Central Ave, Cheyenne, WY 82001

ISBN-13:978-1492721758

ISBN-10: 1492721751

This book is dedicated to every dog I have ever owned and loved.

CONTENTS

CHAPTER ONE

ESCAPE

Charlie Newcomb crouched in front of a bush on the edge of the arrival/departure pad. He was carrying a book that he tucked under his arm for safety. He had read and studied the book over and over. He was thoroughly familiar with it, but he brought it just in case he forgot anything. Charlie had ducked down to hide himself while he caught his breath. He had just run at full speed through the trees and bushes that grew near the pad. He looked around and could see most of his companions. They too, were catching their breath. They too, had carefully hidden themselves while they waited for Charlie to give the signal. When he did, they would stand up and all run as fast as possible for the time craft hanger.

Charlie waited a second to build his courage. He knew he could not wait long. The enemy was too close. He also knew most of his companions were about to die making the run to the hanger.

He could very well be one of the ones gunned down as they crossed the wide, open space. He had to act. If he didn't give the signal soon they would all die where they were.

Charlie stood. "Now," he yelled. He looked over his shoulder. He could see the enemy not far away. He didn't wait to count, but with a glance he could see there were a lot of them. Charlie's friends all started to run at once. They zigged and zagged just as Charlie had taught them, trying not to be an easy target.

Balls of blue light began to fill the air. They did not surprise Charlie. He had seen these balls before, but this time it amazed him how many there were. Some passed close by him. Each one that passed scared him. They were silent and there was no way to hear them coming. He knew what would happen if one of the blue balls hit him. He told himself not to worry about the ones he could see. It was the one he did not see that would end his life.

Blue balls were hitting some of his friends. There was no noise when that happened. Death was so fast, the people did not even scream. Charlie just heard the thump as each body hit the ground. He kept running. He knew the worst thing he could do was to turn and see who had been downed. He forced himself to think only about his goal. He had to get to the hanger. If he was hit, someone else had to get to the hanger in his stead.

Charlie's friends all knew why they had been chosen for this suicide mission. Each one was good at math. Charlie had tested them all and he had selected those able to answer math questions the fastest. He said they had the aptitude.

He had read to them from the book he was carrying. It was an old time craft instruction manual. He had memorized the book and then taught them all exactly what to do. If they were lucky enough to get to the hanger they had to get inside the building. There, they had to find the remotes and they had to speak the answers to the math questions that appeared on the remotes. That should open the doors on some of the time craft. They had to jump into a craft and answer the question they saw on the screen in the craft's front wall. That would close the door and a small keypad would appear. They knew exactly what sequence and frame to enter on the keypad. Each one had memorized the setting by heart. They had practiced and practiced until they could enter the setting in their sleep. The question was, could they enter it while under fire?

Charlie heard more thumps as more bodies fell to the ground. His chest hurt. He was running as fast as he could. He and everyone else on the pad had practiced sprinting for weeks. They were in the best shape possible. Still, his legs felt like he was in slow motion. He had had nightmares like this. In his dreams his legs were like cement and he could barely move them.

Charlie's heart pounded and his face felt hot. Thump. Thump. More bodies fell. At this rate Charlie wondered if anyone would be alive to make it to the door. He could see the goal getting closer and he forced his legs to yield every bit of strength they had. Thump. Another friend fell.

Finally, Charlie reached the door and several friends joined him. They too had survived the run across the pad. Now they faced a problem they had not expected. The door was locked. They all backed up and threw their shoulders against the door. Thump. One of them fell in a burst of blue light. Other friends arrived. Thump. Another fell. The group clustered around the door made an easy target.

The door groaned as the group of people pushed against it. Another burst of light. Thump. Finally, the lock gave way and the door opened. Thump. Another friend fell into the open door way. Charlie grabbed her arm and dragged her body inside. He had to get her out of the way so the door could close. The few people still alive slammed the door and leaned against it. They would try to hold it long enough for Charlie to find the remotes.

The people felt a heavy force hit the door. It shook. "We can't hold off the Dandelions very long," one of them yelled. "Hurry, Charlie."

Charlie ran behind a long row of time craft, all covered with dust. No one had been here in years. He stopped to open some drawers. He ran to some cabinets and opened them. At last, he found the remotes all lined up neatly on a shelf. He grabbed one and read the panel; *64 plus 18,* it read.

"Eight-two," Charlie yelled. A door opened on one of the time craft and Charlie ran back down the row to reach that craft. He saw his friends still struggling to keep the door closed. They were losing. The door was open a crack. A yellow hand reached inside. A friend hit it with a hammer.

Charlie jumped into the craft. He read the problem on the wall panel and the door closed. A small key pad came silently out of the wall. Charlie hit the keys. He knew the sequence and frame, but his brain was swirling. He fumbled as he tried to enter it and had to start all over again.

Outside, the door had been forced open a bit more. Another yellow hand reached in. This one was holding a weapon. A blue ball dropped one of the people pushing on the door. Without that person's weight and strength, the door opened even more. Another blue ball dropped another person, the rest quickly followed.

The door burst open and large, yellow figures forced their way in. The figures were much taller than the people dead on the floor. They had no features. Anyone still alive would have thought the figures looked like a cross between a robot and a knight in armor. More of the figures came through the door until the hanger was full of them. They walked up and down the row of time craft examining each one to see if anyone was hiding there.

Suddenly, one of the craft in the middle of the long row disappeared, leaving an empty space where it had once been parked. Several blue balls collided in the empty space. They were too late. A craft with someone in it had escaped.

The yellow figures grabbed any tools they could find and began to beat the remaining time craft. It was obvious they wanted to destroy them. The crafts' tough hulls did not even dent. One of the yellow figures picked up a laser saw and tried it. The hull sliced as cleanly as if it were butter.

The figures set about cutting all the craft into pieces. As they did they threw the pieces about the hanger. They did not stop until every craft had been destroyed. Then, the commander gave a signal and the yellow figures formed a row. The long row began to leave the hanger, following the leader. As they walked out they stepped in several puddles of goo on the floor near the door and on the step outside. The puddles were quickly tracked all over. However, before they were spread around by many dozens of yellow feet, the puddles had the outlines of human bodies.

CHAPTER TWO

SHADOW DAY

The eighth grade class at Atlantic Academy waited in line in the gym. They were wearing their school uniforms. The boys wore white shirts and black pants. They all had the Atlantic Academy school tie. The girls were in gray slacks or gray skirts with white blouses. It was May, so most of the shirts and blouses had short sleeves.

This was Shadow Day and the eighth grade was visiting Atlantic Academy high school. There, each student would be matched with a ninth grader and the younger student would "shadow" the older. That meant going to classes, lunch, and gym together. Shadow Day let Atlantic Academy's eighth graders learn their way around the high school and experience life as a freshman.

Patrick Weaver, Nick Pope, and Mike Castleton stood together in line with their class. The three had been best friends since the second grade. They were about to turn 14. They had all grown and changed this past year. Nick had always been short and thin. He was now the tallest kid in the eighth grade, but he was still very skinny. The other kids had nicknamed him *Beanpole*. His mother had trouble finding clothes for him. Most stores did not carry clothes long enough for his limbs, but small enough for his thin body. Nick's hair still wouldn't behave and he looked like he had a permanent case of helmet hair. He still looked like he was perpetually worried. He wasn't. That was just his normal expression.

Mike had grown too, but was a lot shorter than Nick. Mike's eyes were still deep blue. They had thick eyebrows and long, dark lashes. Mike's freckles had begun to fade. Most important for Mike, his face had gotten longer and his ears laid more against his head. When he was younger, Mike's ears stuck out and his head was round like a soccer ball. His father called him Charlie Brown.

Patrick had light-blue eyes and sandy hair. The freckles on his nose had finally faded away. Patrick was the shortest of the three. However, he was still the heaviest. He was not fat, just strong. Patrick had recently earned a black belt in Tae-Kwon-Do. All that training had made him very muscular. The other eighth graders called him *Fireplug*.

"What did you do this weekend?" Patrick asked Nick. He was just making conversation while the class waited.

"My grandpa and I put a supercharger on a 1967 GTO," Nick said.

"A what?" Patrick asked.

"A GTO. It was one of the first muscle cars," Nick answered. "Muscle cars had really big, powerful V-eight engines. They were used for drag racing. My grandpa had one when he was a kid. He's really excited to have another one."

"What's a supercharger," Mike asked.

"It's a blower that sits on top of the engine and pushes air into it. The extra air makes the engine even more powerful without burning more gasoline. So, you get the same mileage, but more power.

"We took the GTO out to the drag strip in Lee. My father drove the car and I rode shotgun. The car was so powerful he burned rubber in all four gears. The GTO is so fast I was pushed back in my seat while we accelerated. When I looked back down the drag strip there was nothing but a cloud of blue smoke from the tires. It was really awesome.

"My father let me drive the GTO, but I had to keep it slow. I can't wait until the day when he lets me really open up that supercharged V-eight."

Patrick and Mike were impressed. They hadn't even started driving lessons yet and Nick was burning rubber on a drag strip.

"What did you do, Mike?" Patrick asked his other friend.

"I did the research for my English term paper," Mike said. "We read the *Red Badge of Courage* this term. It's a book about this soldier in the Civil War. We have to do a research paper about life back then. You know the people in the South really had it bad. The South's biggest business was growing cotton, so they didn't build factories to make a lot of stuff. That meant they had to buy everything from other countries. The north blocked all the ports and ships couldn't bring in all the goods the south needed.

"You'll like this one," Mike said. "The south couldn't get gunpowder. So, it had to make its own. Gunpowder is really simple. It's just sulfur, charcoal, and saltpeter. They got the saltpeter by making everyone collect their pee. Everybody had to save their pee and let it dry to get the saltpeter. The soldiers got the bullets and gunpowder wrapped up in little paper packages called cartridges. When they loaded their guns they tore the paper cartridge with their teeth. How would you like to be a soldier biting open a cartridge knowing someone's pee was in the gunpowder?" The boys all had a good laugh.

At that point, Miss Watson, the Atlantic Academy grade school principal walked into the gym with the high school headmaster, Mr. Gibson. Miss Watson was a small woman. Mr. Gibson was not a big man, but he was a giant next to Miss Watson. Except for a couple of girls, all the kids in the eighth grade were bigger than the tiny principal.

Even though they were bigger, the eighth graders feared Miss Watson. When she spoke they always looked at the ground, never directly at her. "This is your last year with me," Miss Watson told the class. "Next year, you will be in the high school and Mr. Gibson will be your headmaster. I trust you will all remember how I have taught you to behave. I trust that you will always be polite and well-spoken. I trust you will never embarrass me or the grade school. Now, go with Mr. Gibson and have a good day shadowing the ninth grade."

Mr. Gibson stepped to the front of the line. "Please follow me," he said. He led the eighth grade across the campus to the high school. The students followed him into the high school lobby where they found the ninth grade waiting for them. Each ninth grader had a name badge pinned to his or her uniform. The high school wore the same uniform as the junior high, but they also had blue blazers.

Teachers sat at tables with name badges lined up in front of them. "A through F here," Mr. Gibson said pointing at a table. "G through Z there." He pointed at another table. The eighth grade lined up to get their name badges and find out who they would shadow.

When the eighth and ninth graders were all matched Mr. Gibson called them to attention. "I run the high school," he said. "Unlike Miss Watson, I do not deal with discipline. The assistant headmaster has that job. You will all be happy to know I will have a new assistant headmaster next year," he announced. "I believe you all know her. In fact, some of you may even have had her as a teacher."

Patrick, Nick, and Mike gasped. Mrs. Martin stepped forward and stood next to Mr. Gibson. They knew Mrs. Martin. For some reason Mrs. Martin disliked the three boys and did everything she could to make them miserable. She still held a grudge because they had embarrassed her when they were in the sixth grade. It happened during Open House when Mrs. Martin's CD player wouldn't work. The boys had played a live version of the school hymn, even though they had been told not to.

Now, Mrs. Martin was in charge of discipline. The boys knew she would use all her authority to get even with them. They each made a silent pledge to stay as far away from her as possible.

At the end of the school day the eighth grade returned to the lobby. Now, even more tables were set up in there. Representatives of all the high school clubs, the newspaper, and the band were at the tables. The representatives explained their club activities to the eighth graders and invited them to join.

The athletic coaches were also in the lobby. They were looking over the eighth graders and searching for new talent for their teams. The football coach zeroed in on Patrick. He looked at the student's name tag and said, "Mr. Weaver, you look like a really good tackle. Have you ever played football? If not, don't worry. We'll teach you."

"I do martial arts," Patrick answered.

"Great," the coach replied. "That means you're not afraid of contact. I'll bet you know how to take down a running back. Look, we have a football camp in August before school starts. Why don't you come and try it? I can guarantee you'll be first string. You'll play every game."

"Let me think about it," Patrick said. "I'll have to talk to my parents."

"Here, take this," the coach said as he gave Patrick a loose leaf binder. "It's our football team's play book," the coach explained. "Look it over. It'll help when you start camp. You'll already know the plays."

"Can I have one too, Coach?" Mike asked. "I've been thinking I would like to play football."

"Yeah, sure kid," the coach said. He gave Mike a play book without even looking at him. "See you in August, Mr. Weaver." He waved goodbye to Patrick.

Patrick and Mike followed Nick as he approached the hockey coach. "Sir, I would like to join the hockey team. I played goalie for four years."

The coach looked at Nick and began to laugh. "You don't look like any goalie I've ever seen," the coach said. "You're so skinny a good breeze could blow you away. The puck would probably knock you over."

"I've played goalie," Nick added. "But I've always wanted to be a wingman. I'm really accurate with a puck."

The coach laughed at Nick again. "You'd end up in the next county every time you got checked." The coach looked at Nick's name tag. "The way you're built Pope, go see the basketball coach." He laughed again.

Nick walked off in a huff. "He wouldn't even let me show what I could do," he complained.

"I learned something from the girl I shadowed," Patrick told his friends. "We've always called Atlantic Academy *Double A*, because of its initials, AA. The high school calls the place *A Squared*. The freshmen all take algebra. In algebra AA means A multiplied by A. That equals A squared."

Mr. Gibson waited until the activity at the tables had dropped off. "Eighth grade," he said loudly to get everyone's attention. "It will only take you a few more minutes to finish speaking with club representatives. When you are done you are moving on to the cafeteria for supper. After supper we will all gather in the gym with the ninth graders for the mixer dance. It is my understanding the music will be provided by your very own band, the Sirens."

At the mention of the Sirens the eighth graders began to clap. Patrick, Nick, and Mike were the Sirens. They had been playing for the Atlantic Academy grammar and junior high schools since they were in the sixth grade. Patrick was the drummer. Nick played bass. Mike played electric guitar and was the lead singer. Their classmates loved their music and were excited about the evening. It would be their first high school dance. Kids slapped the boys on the back and said encouraging things.

The annual mixer was a dance held at the high school for the ninth grade and the incoming eighth grade. Most of the kids in the two classes knew each other, as they had only been a year apart through grade school. This gave them a chance to catch up on old times and form some bonds that would last through high school.

Mrs. Martin slowly worked her way over to where the boys were standing and stood beside Patrick. After a moment she began to speak. She never looked at the boys, so other people would think she just happened to be standing next to them. "This is the last time the Sirens will play at Atlantic Academy," she said. "I don't start my new job until next year. Then, I'm the one who will be making these decisions. I don't know why Miss Watson has been protecting you, but she won't be around anymore. Enjoy tonight. Your playing days are over.

"By the way," she added. "I'm a stickler about the dress code. Mr. Weaver, keep your shoes shined next year. Mr. Pope, keep your hair combed. Mr. Castleton, keep your tie tight. Don't give me any excuse to come down on you, because I will. You don't have anyone to protect you now."

The boys grimaced as Mrs. Martin walked away. "I still don't know what she has against us," Nick said.

"Hello, A Squared," Mike yelled into the microphone. "We are the Sirens and I'm Captain Mike." He was wearing his signature captain's hat. His guitar hung from his shoulder by its fuzzy, hot-pink strap. "Thanks for inviting us to play at your dance. This is a mixer. So, we're going to mix things up a bit. We're going to mix in some of our own songs. See if you can tell the difference."

Mike turned to look at Patrick and Nick. Patrick tapped out the rhythm on the edge of a drum and Mike began playing and singing. "One, two, three o'clock, four o'clock, rock. Five, six, seven o'clock, eight o'clock, rock…" Kids loved the beat. Some couples ran onto the floor and began to dance. Individual kids slowly worked their way out and danced in groups. Soon, the whole gym was a sea of movement. The kids thought this was a great song with a great beat for dancing. The teachers were surprised and some raised their eyebrows. They recognized this song. It was made famous by Bill Haley and the Comets way back in 1956. Their parents had danced to this song.

Mr. Newcomb, the Atlantic Academy grammar school and junior high music teacher, stood against the gym wall with a big smile on his face. He knew Mike Castleton well enough to realize the trick he had pulled on his classmates. Mr. Newcomb leaned over and told one of the high school teachers, "Those boys are clever. They really like classic Rock 'n Roll. They knew that the other kids wouldn't want to dance to oldies. So, the singer said he was mixing in some of their own music. The kids think the Sirens wrote this song and that it's real cool. They would die if they knew their grandparents danced to it."

As the Sirens finished *Rock around the Clock*, they immediately began another song. Mike started to sing "Way down in Louisiana next to New Orleans, way back in the woods among the evergreens...." The students never stopped dancing. Mike began to duck walk across the stage just like the song's original singer, Chuck Berry. The duck walk is done by leaning back on one heel and hopping with the other leg held out. None of the kids knew who Chuck Berry was, or that he had made the duck walk famous. They thought this was Mike's own move and that it was cool.

Mr. Gibson approached Miss Watson and invited her to dance. Miss Watson is from the future and didn't know how to dance to this type of music, so Mr. Gibson showed her. Pretty soon he had her doing the jitter bug. It was an old way of dancing. The couple faces one another holding hands, and rocks back and forth. The man lifts his hand and the woman spins under their arms and back to face the man. Seeing the grammar school principal and the high school headmaster dance together, other teachers got out on the floor. The kids were surprised when they looked around to discover the chaperones dancing alongside them.

Mike spoke into the microphone. "This is a mixer. So, I want you to mix it up. We're gonna do a slow song for you ladies. Eighth grade ladies, I want you to choose a ninth grade guy. Ninth grade ladies, you have to choose a guy from the eighth grade. Teachers, you can choose among yourselves."

He started to sing in a low voice, "Love me tender, love me true...."

The Sirens played for about an hour. Soaked with sweat, Mike told the crowd the band was going to take a break. As they walked down from the stage a ninth grade girl moved in beside Mike and took him by the arm. "You're awesome," she said. Mike knew why she held his arm. She was laying claim to him and telling all the other girls to keep away. "Are you dating anyone?" she asked in a flirting voice.

"Uh, yeah," Mike answered, thinking fast. "Her name is Allie."

"Oh," said the girl with disappointment and a pout. "What about the tall one?"

"Nick?" Mike asked. "Yeah. His girlfriend's name is Lenore. But, Patrick's available," Mike said with a devilish grin.

"Oh, good," the girl said as she walked away. She grabbed Patrick's arm, just as she had Mike's. The drummer looked shocked. He didn't have any interest in girls yet. Mike knew the girl had just asked him if he had a girlfriend and that Patrick didn't know what to do. Mike waited for Nick to catch up with him and the two laughed at the joke Mike had played on their friend. Patrick had always teased them about Allie and Lenore. Mike had just evened the score.

The dance ended at 9:00. Shadow Day is a homework-free day. Still, both grades had to be back for classes in the morning. The boys remained behind packing their instruments and amplifiers. The ninth grade girl had come up on the stage with them, still flirting with Patrick. She left after giving Patrick her cell phone number and email address. "Friend me," she said as she walked away.

The Social Studies teacher Mr. Smith climbed the stage stairs. "Good job, gentlemen," he said to the boys. "Your classmates really seemed to like your music."

"Thank you, Sir," Patrick said. He stopped packing and shook the teacher's hand.

"You three are scheduled to teach classes at the Time Institute before the end of the term," Mr. Smith said. "Have you thought about when you'll do it?'

"We've been pretty swamped with work lately," Mike said. "I forgot about it."

"How about this weekend?" Patrick offered. "If we leave on Saturday morning and return to that frame, we'll still have time to get all our homework done. We can tell our parents we are taking a walk in the woods so they won't miss us. Time travel messes with your mind and I find I need to adjust when I get back. It's tough to work a long time at the Institute and have to be back in school the next day."

"Let's do this," Mr. Smith added. "I'll have Miss Watson excuse you from your last classes of the day on Friday afternoon.

You can go then. You'll be back in time to meet your parents at the end of the school day. That way, you'll have the whole weekend to yourselves so you can adjust. Most important, you won't have to mislead your parents."

The boys all agreed with the plan. In fact, it was a good deal. It meant skipping out on the last class of the day and having their weekend free. "I will take my craft to the woods where you keep the CT 9225," Mr. Smith explained. "Then, I will take your craft to the Institute and its frame of origination. It's been almost a year since you were last there. So, I'll have lots of time to spend with Mrs. Smith and I'll be home for all of Lenore's cadet term. You know she started her training not long after your last visit. In fact, she'll be in the classes you teach. So, you'll get to see her again.

"I'll leave the Institute a couple of days before your classes are scheduled to begin and return here in the CT 9225. That will give it a new frame of origination so you arrive a couple of days before you begin teaching. I'm sure you have things you want to prepare

"I've been watching you this year," Mr. Smith continued. "You've grown and gotten heavier. I don't know if you can all travel in the CT 9225 together. Mr. Weaver, you may have to take Mr. Pope and Mr. Castleton one at a time."

The boys looked at each other and then at themselves. This was a new realization. Together, they weighed more than a time craft could carry. "Yeah," Patrick said. "That is a problem. Our time traveling days may be over."

CHAPTER THREE
TIME CRAFT SUPERCHARGER

The boys met at the end of the second-floor hallway, outside the door to the roof. The last class of the day had begun and all the teachers and students were in the classrooms. Mike had brought a guitar and amplifier with him. "What are those for?" Patrick asked.

"Sometimes I get bored when I'm at the Institute," Mike answered. "I brought these along to keep myself busy. Maybe I'll write some new songs while we're there."

"We're worried about weight and you bring a guitar and amplifier?" Patrick asked. "That's pretty dumb. If they put us over our weight limit you're leaving them on the roof." Mike ignored him.

Mr. Smith opened the door and signaled the waiting boys to follow him to the roof. There, he gave Patrick the remote to the CT 9225 and the pilot and his engineer went into their craft to change. A minute later they came back out carrying their Fixer uniforms. "We have another problem," Patrick said to Mr. Smith." He and Nick held up their uniforms. Patrick's was far too small to fit around his muscular body. Nick's uniform pants ended way above his ankles. "Pretty safe bet yours doesn't fit either," Patrick said to Mike.

"Hum," Mr. Smith said out loud. "This is not good." He thought for a moment and concluded, "You'll have to travel in your Atlantic Academy uniforms. Fortunately, you are only going to another sequence and frame. You don't have to go into space.

"Time crew uniforms are all one size. That's because the crews are all one size – small. When you get to the Institute, talk with Dr. Newcomb or Rabbi Cohen. They'll have to arrange for a tailor to make you new uniforms."

Mike and Mr. Smith watched the CT 9225's door close on Patrick and Nick. It reopened and Patrick was alone. Mike climbed in with his guitar and amplifier. "You're lucky this time, Mike," Patrick said as he looked at the weight indicator on the control panel. "You have two pounds to spare. You won't be bringing those along next year. We'll have grown even more."

"We'll see you on Monday morning," Mike said to Mr. Smith before Patrick closed the door. "This will be a routine visit. We've taught these classes before."

The boys arrived at the MacDonald Center to find Dr. Newcomb's *Ethics of Time Travel* class had just ended. The group cadets had left Dr. Newcomb's room and were arriving in Rabbi Cohen's classroom. Dr. Newcomb stepped out of his classroom and started down the hall towards his office. As he walked past the boys he glanced at them and began to say "Good morn...." He stopped in middle of the word when he realized who they were. "Mr. Weaver, Mr. Pope, Mr. Castleton what happened to you?" Then he understood. "My, you have all grown," he said with surprise. "Time travel does mess with your mind. Why are you not in uniform?" he asked, still startled by how much the boys had changed.

"Good morning, Dr. Newcomb," Patrick said shaking the teacher's hand. "It's good to see you again. Yes, I'm afraid we've grown and our uniforms don't fit anymore. Mr. Smith said you would find a tailor to make us new ones. We should be dressed in Fixer uniforms when we teach. These are our school clothes from Atlantic Academy. I don't think they are appropriate here at the Institute."

"Yes. Yes, I can get a tailor," Dr. Newcomb said. "Will you excuse me for just a moment? I want to tell Rabbi Cohen you are here. I'll ask him to join us in my office when he finishes his *History of Time Travel* class."

The tailor was measuring the boys for their new uniforms when Rabbi Cohen arrived at Dr. Newcomb's office. He greeted the boys with enthusiasm. "So, it's time for you to teach your classes to the new cadets? I'm sure they will all benefit."

"How long are you staying?" Dr. Newcomb asked. "I'll tell you why I want to know. Prof. Garcia from the University of New Hampshire has requested a research mission. He asked specifically that you boys make it for him. I know you're Fixers and not Researchers. However, the mission will be tricky, as it involves more danger than usual. You three have faced danger before and proven you are resourceful."

"That will be a problem," Patrick said with a grimace. "We weigh too much to fly together in a time craft. I brought Mike and Nick here one at a time. I'm afraid our days as a Fixer team are over."

"That is too bad," said Dr. Newcomb with concern. "You were such a valuable crew. I hate to lose you."

"It is too bad," Rabbi Cohen repeated. "I'm afraid there is a limit on the amount of weight a time craft can move at hyper-light speed. In total, a craft can weight no more than 400 pounds. We learned this long ago. There is no way to increase the power."

Nick was silent and had a strange, far-away look in his eyes. The two teachers noticed his expression and stared at him. Patrick and Mike saw the teachers staring and turned to look at Nick too. "Nick," Patrick asked. "Are you all right?"

"Huh?" Nick said as he came out of his daydream.

"Are you all right?" Patrick repeated.

"Yeah," Nick answered. "Yeah. I'm fine. Dr. Newcomb I've had an idea. I'm going to the lab. I'll need some help. Can you get Lenore Smith excused from her classes for the rest of the day? And, tomorrow too?" he added.

"She's excused from my class," Dr. Newcomb replied. "Yours too, Rabbi?" Rabbi Cohen nodded. "I'll take care of her other classes," Dr. Newcomb told Nick. "Do you want to tell Miss Smith, or shall I?"

"I'll do it," Nick said. "If I leave now I can probably catch her as she leaves her *Time Craft Mechanics* class. We can go to the lab and get right to work. I'll see you guys at the crew quarters tonight," he said to Mike and Patrick. "Do we still have the same apartment?" he asked Dr. Newcomb. The teacher nodded and Nick ran out the door.

"You gentlemen will be interested in the latest news about some of your friends," Rabbi Cohen said to Patrick and Mike. "Miss Tymoshenko made a good recovery. She's working again and has completed several missions since she returned to the Institute. Miss Canfield has also decided to continue working here. She is due back in a couple of days. You'll get to see her before you leave for home."

Mike and Patrick thanked the teachers and excused themselves. "I'll have your new uniforms delivered to your quarters this afternoon," Dr. Newcomb said.

Mike stood outside the door to Allie's quarters. He could hear music coming from inside. It was no surprise that Allie was listening to music. She was a Researcher and specialized in music history. Mike paused a minute to listen as well. He knew a lot about music too. Still, he didn't recognize what he heard. It sounded strangely familiar but he couldn't put his finger on it. He knew it was possible the music was written after his time.

He knocked and waited. He could hear someone walking inside. Allie opened the door and gasped in surprise to see her friend Mike Castleton standing outside her apartment. "Mike," she cried as she threw her arms around his neck and kissed his cheek. "I'm so glad to see you. Come in," she said as she took him by the hand. "Tell me you're staying for a while. Don't let this be a short visit."

"Patrick, Nick, and I are back to teach at the Institute," Mike said. "We're staying for several days. When I'm not in the classroom I want to spend every minute with you. I really missed you, Allie. I think about you every day." Entering the room Mike noticed with surprise that Allie bore a large scar on her cheek in the shape of the letter F. "Allie," he said. "Your brand. You still have it. Dr. Newcomb said you were better."

"I am better, Mike," Allie answered. "I am better and I can work again. However, time travel messes with your mind. My time as Demetrius' slave is still part of me. Maybe it always will be.

The scar reminds me that there really is evil in the world, and that I saw evil win over and over. I'm afraid I have to keep the scar until I see that evil can be beaten. I need to see evil lose."

Mike hugged her again. "I love you, Allie Tymoshenko," he said. "I see the inner you, and you are the most beautiful person I know. What you have on your cheek doesn't make you any less beautiful in my eyes. That's why I wear this," he said, pulling a gold heart-shaped locket from under his uniform shirt and opening it. Allie remembered the locket. She had given it to Mike moments before he left on his first mission. When the mission was completed Mike would return to his own time, and the two did not know if they would ever see each other again. That's why Allie had engraved *Remember Me* on the cover. She looked at the picture as Mike extended the open locket toward her. She had a vivid memory of when it was taken. They were in the cadet dorm common room one evening studying when her roommate pointed a camera at the pair. Mike had put his arm around Allie's shoulder to draw her closer and the two had inclined their heads together so they touched. "I never take off this locket," Mike said seriously. "I shower with it. I sleep with it. You are always next to my heart, Allie. You always will be."

Allie suddenly remembered the music she was playing. She pulled away from Mike and hurried to turn it off. "What was that all about?" Mike asked.

Allie pondered the question. She didn't want to answer it, but knew she had to. "That was the Sirens," she said. "That's a collection of your greatest hits. I listen to your music all the time. It makes me feel close to you. You haven't written those songs yet. They're from your future, and you shouldn't hear them. I don't want to change your sequence."

"It does mess with your mind," Mike replied, regretting he had not listened more closely to the music. Still, he knew it was best to forget what he had heard.

Nick got home late in the evening. Mike, Allie, and Patrick had eaten supper together and were by the pool talking. "What are you working on, Nick?" Patrick asked his exhausted friend. "You look whipped."

"I am," Nick answered. "If everything goes right, I can show you tomorrow. Will you three meet us at the arrival/departure pad at 4:00 in the afternoon? Allie, bring your uniform gloves and head cover. Yours are in the CT 9225," he said to Mike and Patrick as he dragged himself off to bed.

Lenore and Nick were waiting at the CT 9225 when Patrick, Allie, and Mike arrived. Nick had asked the maintenance crews to move the craft out of the hanger onto the pad where he could work on it. "Would you three join Lenore and me inside?" Nick asked. All five climbed into the craft. "Now, Patrick would you close the door?" Patrick gave Nick a questioning look, but did as asked.

"Now, Patrick, would you program in a trip to A Squared? I want to show Lenore and Allie where we go to school."

"Why are you goofing around like this?" Patrick asked, clearly annoyed. "This craft can't carry even the three of us anymore. Never mind five of us."

"Work with me, Patrick," Nick insisted. "Program in a trip to Atlantic Academy." Patrick shrugged and did as Nick asked. "Okay. It's in," he said. "Now what?"

"I want to show Lenore and Allie where we go to school," Nick replied. He knew he was annoying Patrick, but was having fun yanking his friend's chain. Patrick looked really mad. "Okay. Cool down," Nick said. "Notice the knob near the key pad? It's new. See the small screen next to the knob. It's new too. Check the weight indicator for our total weight."

"It's 585 pounds," Patrick said. "The craft's total weight cannot be more than 400 pounds. We can't go anywhere without some of you getting out," the pilot added hotly. He was not enjoying Nick's games. He just wanted Nick to give him a clear explanation of what he was up to.

"Turn the knob until you see 585 on the screen," Nick answered. Patrick did as told. "Now, the CT 9225 can carry 585 pounds. Maybe you should turn the knob to 590, just for good measure."

"Patrick's not taking this well," Mike said to Nick. "Maybe you should just explain what you've done."

"I've put a supercharger on the CT 9225," Nick said. "I increased its power."

"Rabbi Cohen said that was impossible," Mike replied.

"You guys said a universal translator was impossible," Nick answered. "Now, all the time crews have them. Look, I found a way to get more power out of the CT 9225. You know an amplifier takes sound and increases it. I used the same idea to boost the craft's charge so it can carry more weight."

Mike paused a minute while he thought about this. He howled when he realized what had happened. "You did it again. You took my amp." He looked around the craft and spotted parts from his amp wired into the CT 9225. "I told you to stop doing that to me, Nick. Leave my stuff alone. At least ask me before you take it."

Nick ignored Mike. "Patrick, please take the new supercharged CT 9225 on its maiden voyage. Let's show the girls our school." Patrick did as Nick asked. When he opened the door the CT 9225 was on Atlantic Academy's roof. "This is A Squared. This is where we go to school," Nick announced as Lenore and Allie peeked out the door. "That's the playground down below. The soccer field is over there. That's the high school, where we'll go next year," he added, pointing at a larger building across the campus. The girls looked around with curiosity.

"Okay, Patrick," Nick said. "We don't want to take any chances of being seen. Take us back to the Institute."

"No. Wait," Mike said. "Miss Watson would be upset if we didn't act like gentlemen. We should invite the girls to lunch. First, take me to my house. No one's home and I want get another amp. Leave this one alone, Nick," he warned the engineer.

Patrick landed the CT 9225 on the lawn behind Mike's house. "Come on in, Lenore," Mike said. "I'll show you where I live. You can meet my dog, Menlo." As the door opened Menlo ran up to Mike to greet him. Menlo was a Foxhound. He was brown and white with a black forehead and a tail that was half black and half white. That tail was large and powerful. It usually stood straight up and curved over his back like an upside down J. Menlo greeted Patrick and Nick. He was well acquainted with them as he usually slept in the cellar with the Sirens when they practiced. "Mennie, this is Lenore. You remember Allie," Mike said to his dog. Menlo greeted the girls. He sniffed their feet as his strong tail thumped against the refrigerator. Lenore and Allie stooped down and hugged Menlo, who happily lapped their cheeks.

Meanwhile, Mike got his other amplifier from the cellar. As he was about to climb the stairs he paused and grabbed his football and playbook from a shelf. The group walked out to the CT 9225 together. Menlo carried a toy to Lenore so she could throw it for him. "I can make us peanut butter and jelly sandwiches," Mike said. "But I would rather we all have a treat. Patrick, we need to go to Bayonne, New Jersey. We're going to have the best pizza in the world. Pile into the craft, guys."

Mike called Menlo. When the dog realized Mike was going to put him back in the house, he jumped into the CT 9225 with Lenore and Allie. Mike called the dog again, but he refused to leave the craft. "Can't he come with us?" Allie asked, hugging Menlo around the neck. The dog looked at Mike with sad brown eyes. Mike looked at Patrick for his opinion. Patrick shrugged.

He looked next at Nick. "How much does he weight," Nick asked.

"About 70 pounds," Mike answered.

"Carrying that amp and Menlo would be a good test of how much the supercharger can handle," Nick said, thinking aloud. "Let's bring him. Patrick, check the weight indicator and adjust the knob to match it."

"Head to West 46th Street," Mike said. "You're gonna love this pizza."

"How are we gonna pay for it," Patrick asked Mike quietly. "I don't have any money. Do you?"

"It won't cost us anything," Mike answered. "My Uncle Vince owns the place. He'll give us the pizza for free. He'll even visit with us."

Patrick set the CT 9225 down behind a dumpster in a parking lot. "There's his pizza parlor," Mike said pointing across the street. A large neon sign read *Vince's Thin Crust Pizza.* A smaller sign announced, *The best in the world.*

Mike led his friends into the pizza parlor. Inside the door the others looked around the dining area. The walls were covered with pictures of famous people, actors, politicians, and news broadcasters. Many of the pictures had handwritten notes praising the pizza and the owner. All sorts of awards for the best pizza hung along with the pictures. The other four time travelers concluded Mike was right; this was the greatest pizza in the world. After all, lots of famous people agreed with him.

A man with a bald head and a ring of white hair was working behind the counter. He wore wire glasses. The man did a double take as he glanced at the people standing by the door. "Mike? Mike Castleton," the man asked as he recognized his nephew. "Mike. What are you doing here? Are your parents with you?" He came out behind the counter and hugged his nephew and kissed him on the cheek.

"Uncle Vince," Mike said. "These are my classmates Lenore, Allie, Patrick, and Nick. Our team is in town for a math contest. These are our team uniforms. We snuck away to come here. Could you forget to tell my parents we came by?"

Uncle Vince winked at Mike. "Couldn't pass up the pizza, eh? Don't worry. I never saw you. Sit down, all of you. I'll serve you myself. I've got some pizzas coming out of the oven right now. I made them just the way I like them, ultra-thin crust. In fact, I'll have a slice with you. Mike, ask your friends what they want to drink. You know where the sodas are kept."

Mike passed out the drinks and plates as Uncle Vince arrived with two large, round pizzas. The crusts were so thin they looked like huge crackers. Uncle Vince invited Mike's friends to dig in, and each took a slice. Uncle Vince showed them the right way to eat the pizza. He took a slice and folded it like a sandwich.

"Wow." Patrick said. "This is good. The sauce is incredible."

"Yeah," Nick said. "This is the best pizza I've ever had."

Lenore and Allie had never eaten pizza before, but they too agreed it was good.

Uncle Vince reached into his pocket and took out a pill case. He popped a tablet into his mouth and began to eat his slice. "He's lactose intolerant," Mike explained to his friends. "He likes his own pizza so much he takes pills so he can eat it."

"I love this sauce," Patrick repeated.

"That's the secret," Uncle Vince said, winking at Patrick. "The secret's in the sauce. Do you want to know what it is?" Everyone nodded. "Anchovies," Uncle Vince said with a grin.

"Ugh. I hate anchovies," Nick said. Patrick nodded in agreement.

"Everyone hates anchovies," Uncle Vince replied with a self-satisfied grin. "At least everyone thinks they hate anchovies. That's why I grind them up before I put them in the sauce. That's the secret ingredient that makes everyone love my pizza. They'd never try it if I told them it had anchovies in it. So, I don't tell them. I just let them love the taste."

Each time traveler had another slice and finished their drinks. "Uncle Vince," Mike said. "I hate to eat and run, but we gotta get back before we're missed." His uncle nodded in understanding. "Remember, my mom and dad can't know I was here. So, I guess you can't tell Aunt Bobbie either. You know she and my mom talk all the time." He stood up and hugged his uncle.

"Wait," Uncle Vince told him. He boxed the remaining pizza and gave it to Mike. "Just in case you kids get hungry on the trip home. It's a long bus ride to Hampton."

Back in the CT 9225 Allie broke up a slice of pizza and fed it to Menlo. "I proved the supercharger works," Nick said. "Later, I'll do some more experiments to see what its maximum load is. Right now, the important thing is we're back in business." Imitating a New Jersey accent, he added, "Whatdaya say we go tell Dr. Newcomb and Rabbi Cohen and find out about that mission they have for us?"

CHAPTER FOUR
BOWS AND ARROWS

The boys arrived at Room 307 in the MacDonald center on time for their 9:00 appointment. The adults stood to greet them and Dr. Newcomb made the introductions. "Prof. Garcia, this is our team: Mr. Weaver the pilot, Mr. Pope the engineer, and Mr. Castleton the S/O. Gentlemen, this is Prof. Garcia, a well-known historian from UNH who specializes in the European Middle Ages. He has requested a research mission and has asked that you be the team that does it for him.

Prof. Garcia spoke. "Thank you for agreeing to meet with me. Like everyone else at UNH, I know your reputations for being innovative and courageous. That's why I requested you, even though I know you are Fixers and not Researchers. This mission will require someone who can think on the spot and innovate. There is also the possibility of danger."

"We came back to the Institute to teach courses on innovation and self-defense," Patrick said. "We hadn't planned on anything like this, but we'll listen to your request."

"Good," Prof. Garcia replied. "I am studying the English longbow and the changes it caused in medieval warfare."

"The what?" Nick asked.

"The English longbow," Prof. Garcia repeated. "Until the invention of gunpowder most armies used bows and arrows as weapons. The Welsh are a people who live in the southwest corner of England. They developed a bow that was so long it was taller than the archers who used it. It was a very powerful weapon. The Welsh used it successfully when fighting against the English. The English were clever and hired Welsh bowmen to serve in their armies. In time, the English themselves learned how to make and shoot the longbow. They used the weapon in many important battles and won most of them.

"An arrow from a longbow would pierce light amour. Needing more protection from theses arrows, knights began to wear heavier amour. This thicker amour was made or iron, which is softer than steel. In response, the English developed harder steel arrowheads that would punch through the new, heavier amour. So, you can see the longbow changed how battles were fought.

"The longbow became so important to English armies that the kings passed laws requiring that every man learn how to use them. By law, every village had to hold target practice on Sunday afternoons. After church, the whole village would go to the target range, called the butts, and watch the men practice. It was sort of a village picnic.

"The longbow was such an important weapon a lot of people were needed to make all those bows and arrows used by the English army. Special craftsmen made the bows and other craftsmen made the arrows. Some villages had lots of these craftsmen. As you can guess, the villages that made longbows were important places to English kings."

"Did Robin Hood use a longbow?" Nick asked.

"Robin Hood was not a real person," Prof. Garcia explained. "But yes, in the stories he used a longbow. The Robin Hood legend does have some truth to it. There were a lot of skilled bowmen like Robin Hood. They practiced every week with the bow and they were very accurate. They could hit targets at incredible distances. An archer could shoot an arrow two hundred yards."

"That's two football fields," Mike said in amazement.

"Yes," Prof. Garcia agreed. "It's such a long distance it is hard to see a man that far away. So, in the beginning of a battle when the armies were far apart archers shot their arrows in a high arc, into distant groups of soldiers. Arrows fell like rain from the sky, hitting men at random. These were called volleys.

"At short distances, such as across a football field, an archer could target an individual man and hit him. These were called aimed shots. So, at both long and short distances the longbow was deadly. This created a problem for enemy soldiers armed with swords and spears; the archers mowed them down before they got close enough to fight.

"Part of my research is to study the craft of bow and arrow making," Prof. Garcia said. "I want you to meet the craftsmen and ask them questions about their work. I want you to learn about Sunday target practice in the butts. To do this, you will have to speak with these people. You are the only time crew that has ever talked with people in the past. You met and talked to people in the Roman Empire."

The boys liked the idea of this mission. It would be exciting to meet men like Robin Hood. It would be exciting to watch them shooting at the targets. They forgot that Prof. Garcia had also warned there could be danger.

"That part of the mission will be an adventure," Prof. Garcia added. "Now, the second part of my research. In 1415, the English King Henry went to France with an army of about 7,000 men. Most were archers. Months later, after a long march, Henry had run out of food. His men were sick and he was taking his army home. At a place named Agincourt, an army of 20,000 French knights trapped Henry on a narrow field with woods on both sides. He had no escape. The English were outnumbered three to one. They were sick, hungry, and tired. They should have been wiped out by the bigger French army. However, the opposite happened. The longbow archers mowed down the French knights and won what seemed like an impossible battle.

"I am asking you to go to the Battle of Agincourt and observe the longbow being used as a weapon. Here's the danger. There will be thousands of arrows flying. Knights on horses will be charging around the field. If you are close enough to watch the battle, you could get hit by an arrow, or run over by a horse.

"Even if you are not hurt, you need to be prepared for the horrible things you will see. The battle was terrible. History describes piles of dead French knights."

Patrick looked at his teammates. Nick and Mike both nodded enthusiastically. "We'll do it," Patrick told Prof. Garcia.

"Good," Dr. Newcomb answered. "We can give you some help getting there. Mappers have recorded King Henry's sequence. It's in the directory. Finding a village where longbows and arrows are made will be more difficult. We suggest you begin your search with another frame on the king's sequence. Henry V was crowned king of England in 1413. That frame is only two years before the battle. If you go to it, you should be able to find a village where longbows are made. It is even possible archers from such a village would march with Henry in France."

"Correct me if I am wrong, Prof. Garcia," Rabbi Cohen added. "I believe the English of this time spoke a different version of the language than we do."

"You are correct, Rabbi," Prof. Garcia answered. "The English people of 1415 spoke what is called Middle English. We cannot understand the language. The team will have to program its translator helmets." When the team had gone to Rome Nick had developed a helmet that translated a foreign language into English. It also translated the wearer's English into that language. The helmets allowed the team to converse with the people they met in the Roman Empire. Programming the helmets required leaving them in a busy place for three days where they could hear the new language being spoken. When the team arrived in 1415 England their first job would be to take care of this. They had learned that a busy marketplace was a good location for programming.

The boys returned to the crew quarters and told Allie and Lenore that they had accepted the mission. "We won't be long," Mike told Allie. "Would you take care of Menlo for me? He seems to like you as much as I do."

"We'll be fine," Allie said. "I'm worried about you. Promise me you'll be careful."

The CT 9225 came in low over a large English church. There was a celebration going on that had attracted an enormous crowd. It was occurring during a snow storm, making it hard for the boys to see clearly. They could make out a lot of people, a lot of soldiers, and a lot of banners. "That has to be Henry's coronation," Mike said. "We have arrived at the right frame. We need to find a village that makes longbows. Then, we'll have to program the helmets."

"It will be easier to program the helmets in a city," Nick suggested. "There are more people in a city than in a village. We need a place where there are people hanging out all the time, and they need them to be talking about lots of different things. That's how the helmets learn best."

"If it's lots of people you want, there are plenty of them down below," Patrick added. "We did real well in Carthage and in Alexandria leaving the helmets in a market. We should be able to find one here, wherever we are?"

"That's London," Mike said. "We just flew over Westminster Abby. It snows and rains a lot in London and that creates a problem for us. All the buildings here have peaked roofs and we can't set down on them. We'll have to find a place on the ground to land."

Patrick spotted a market near the river. He put his craft down near a bridge and the boys carried the CT 9225 under the overhang to hide it. That night they snuck out with their uniforms cloaked, hid the helmets, and went back to their craft to wait three days. Meanwhile, the people in the market talked away, all their conversations programming the hidden helmets. Three nights later the boys snuck out again to retrieve them.

The next morning the boys walked out from under the bridge in full view of the people in the market. "We've got to find someone who knows where longbows are made," said Patrick.

"I think I see the guy," Mike replied, pointing at a group of soldiers approaching a tavern. The boys watched the men sit at a table and order ale. The tavern owner brought it to them in big leather mugs with handles. "Let them finish their drinks," Mike said. "It will loosen them up and make them less suspicious."

"We don't want them to drink too much," Patrick warned. "Remember those drunks in Carthage. They taught us that too much alcohol makes people stupid. They don't understand our questions, and we don't understand their answers."

The soldiers finished their first round of drinks and called for more. The tavern owner brought them their second tankards. "This is a good time," Mike said. He walked up to one soldier and said, "Excuse me, Captain. Could you settle a bet between me and my friend?"

"I'm a sergeant," the soldier answered.

"I'm sorry for the mistake," Mike said "You look like an important man. I figured you must be a captain."

The soldier's companions laughed and the sergeant looked proud.

"Could you settle our bet? My friend and I have been arguing over which village makes the best longbows." The sergeant examined Mike's uniform with a quizzical expression. "We're Irish squires," Mike explained as the sergeant eyed Nick and Patrick. "Our lord dresses all his squires in this uniform."

That satisfied the man's curiosity. He was a soldier. He understood the importance of uniforms in distinguishing officers from enlisted men, and friend from foe. "I know a lot about longbows," the sergeant said, wiping the ale off his upper lip with his sleeve. "I've seen them used in battles. The best longbows come from the town of Hilton, over near Wales. The boyers, fletchers, and smiths are very good people. They can get lots of yew."

"Lots of me?" Mike asked. "Are those the families that live in Hilton?"

The sergeant looked puzzled at Mike's questions. They didn't make sense.

"How would I find Hilton?" Mike asked, changing the subject. "How would I get there?"

"It's near the border," the sergeant said. "You will have to take the road to Wales. That's it there," he said pointing. "over that bridge toward the west. It's about a three day walk.

"Stop at Hilton. Don't go any farther or you'll end up in Wales. Then, you won't understand anybody. They speak Welsh. Strangest language. It sounds like they're sneezing and gagging at the same time. The Frenchies, at least it sounds like they're trying to talk when you hear them. *Pahlee voo? Wee.*" The other soldiers laughed at the sergeant's imitation of French. Mike winced at the way he butchered the language.

"Are there any signs that will tell us when we get to Hilton," Mike asked.

"No. No signs," the sergeant said. "You don't need any."

"How will I know when I get there," Mike asked, getting a little annoyed.

"You'll see the town up on the hill. That's why they call it Hilton." The sergeant replied. He was getting annoyed too.

"Who makes the bows and arrows, the Boyers, the Fletchers, or the Smiths?" Mike asked.

"They all do," the sergeant said with a puzzled look on his face. Mike didn't understand, but he knew better than to press his luck. The sergeant was becoming unhappy with all these questions. The S/O signaled to Nick and Patrick to head back to the CT 9225.

CHAPTER FIVE
HILTON

From the air Patrick followed the road to Wales. Between villages the road became no more than a narrow wagon trail and was often hard to see through the trees. He was forced to fly low and slow to keep it in sight. "When we get to Hilton we have to find those families that sergeant told us about, the Boyers, the Fletchers, and the Smiths," Mike said.

"Sam Boyer is in our class," Nick noted. "There's a kid named Fletcher in the seventh grade."

"Mr. Smith is our Social Studies teacher," Patrick added. "I wonder if any of them are descended from these families."

The sergeant was right. There was no missing Hilton. It was a large village and it sat on top of a low hill. Patrick landed in some woods and the crew hid the CT 9225 behind some underbrush. The forest was next to a field with a road alongside. The boys crossed the field and followed the road into the village. As they walked they met a man carrying several dead rabbits. He had a longbow over his shoulder and a quiver of arrows on his back.

"Hello," Mike said greeting the archer. "You've had a good hunt."

"My family will be eating rabbit stew tonight," the man said. "I'll stop by my home to give these to my wife and then get to work. Where are you three young men from? I've never seen you in the neighboring villages." Like the sergeant, he looked quizzically at their uniforms.

"We're Irish squires," Mike said. "That's why we're dressed like this. I'm Mike. This is Patrick, and he is Nick. Our lord has made a treaty with your new king to train Irish archers to use the longbow. He has sent us here to see how the bows are made and to learn how to shoot them. We will bring our new knowledge back to our lord so he can help your king."

"You speak very well for Irishmen," The man said. "I know you Irish speak Gaelic, a language like Welsh. We can barely understand the Welsh and Irish when they try to speak English."

"We had an English tutor," Mike said, thinking on his feet.

"So you're squires?" the man asked. "That means you're knights in training. That explains your uniforms and helmets. It also means you're nobles. I need to give you a warning about the longbow. With it a commoner can kill noble knights all afternoon. The French knights hate us. They think it wrong that a man of noble birth should be killed by a commoner. They hate it even more that their knights are not killed in honorable combat, but from far away, by a man they can barely see.

"Do you know what the French do when they capture an English knight? They sell him back to his family for ransom. They make a nice profit. Do you know what they do when they capture an English archer? They cut off the first two fingers of his right hand. He uses those fingers to draw his bow, and without those fingers, the English king has one less archer. When our archers get ready to fight the French, we wave those two fingers at them. We tease the French to come and try to capture us and get our fingers. If we can make the French angry enough to attack, our arrows settle the score for a lot of lost fingers."

"That's the two fingered salute," Mike said. He just realized where this rude gesture had originated. "Doing that with your fingers has the same meaning where we come from. It's a way to say something very unfriendly."

"Our new King Hal is a good and brave warrior," the hunter said. The boys realized Hal was King Henry's nickname, a term of endearment his people used to show their affection for him. "Hal has proved himself in battle and he treats his soldiers kindly. He loves his archers, and we love him. Long live the king! I will help you with your mission because you are here to help my majesty. My name is Tom Littlefield."

"In London we met a soldier who told us to find the Boyers, the Fletchers, and the Smiths in the village of Hilton."

"I'm a bowyer," Tom Littlefield said.

"I thought your name was Littlefield?" Nick asked.

"It is," Tom replied. "I am a bowyer." The boys looked puzzled. The sergeant had not made a lot of sense, but he had clearly said the Boyers, the Fletchers, and the Smiths were the families in Hilton that made longbows. Now, a man named Littlefield had said he came from one of those families.

Tom realized the problem. "You're from Ireland. You don't understand these words. There are English families named Boyer, Fletcher, and Smith. However, a bowyer is a craftsman that makes longbows. A fletcher makes arrows, and a smith makes the steel arrow heads. We have lots of bowyers, fletchers, and smiths, but they all have different family names. We are the best in England. I am a bowyer and I work with other bowyers to make longbows for the king's army."

"I'll bet that's how those family names came about," Mike said to Patrick and Nick. "A long time ago, Joe the bowyer became Joe Boyer."

Fred the fletcher became Fred Fletcher," Nick added.

"I get it," Patrick added. "So kids at school like Amy Carpenter had an ancestor who was a carpenter. Miss Potter the fourth grade teacher had an ancestor who made pots."

"And Patrick Weaver had an ancestor who made cloth," Mike laughed.

"Can we go to work with you, Tom?" Patrick asked. "To learn how bows are made?"

"Walk with me to my cottage," Tom said. "I need to give these rabbits to Mistress Littlefield for supper. Then, we'll all go to the work shed. You'll meet the other bowyers and we'll put you to work. Every boy in this village grows up learning a job that is part of archery. When boys are just beginning to learn a craft we call them apprentices. Every one of us men has had apprentices, so we are experienced at teaching our crafts to others. You will be our apprentices and we will all be your teachers. When you leave here you will be well skilled and ready to bring the longbow to Ireland."

Tom introduced the boys to a group of men working in the shed. They were doing a variety of jobs. Some were seated on a special bench shaving the wood to shape. Others were scraping the bows smooth. Some were wiping oil and wax on the bows.

Another man was working at a small machine like a loom, twisting bow string. Others were applying special tips that looked like plastic, on the ends of the bows. The boys were surprised as plastic would not be invented for another 600 years.

"This is yew," Tom said to the boys holding a long piece of wood. "Us?" Mike asked, confused again.

"No," Tom said. "This piece of wood came from a tree called yew. We have lots of yew near Hilton." At last, Mike understood. The sergeant had been making sense. It was Mike who did not understand. "We choose the best and straightest yew trees. There are some behind the shed. We split the trunk into long pieces called staves." Nick wandered over to look at the trees. Most of the limbs had been cut off, but some small branches were left. "Be careful," Tom warned. "Everything about the yew is poisonous - the leaves, the berries. Everything but the wood. That's only deadly to the Frenchies when it's pulled by a good archer."

"See this stave," Tom said, showing it to the boys. "Here's the secret. The white wood grows just under the bark. It's called sapwood. Sapwood is real springy and wants to stay straight. The dark wood comes from the inside of the tree and is called heartwood. It bends real well. So, we place the dark heartwood on the outside of the bow and white sapwood on the inside. When you pull the string the dark heartwood bends. When you release the string, the white sapwood wants to straighten out. That shoots the arrow. See the shape of this finished bow? The brown outside surface is flat and the white inside surface is rounded.

"We put the bow on this special machine called a tiller," Tom explained, placing his hand on a tiller that had a bow mounted on it. "The tiller makes sure both sides of the bow bend evenly. The upper and lower lengths of the bow are called the limbs." The boys saw how the machine pulled the string and bent the bow like it was in the hands of an archer. This allowed bowyer to stand back and examine the results of his work.

"We fit the ends of the limbs with these specially-shaped pieces of cow horn," Tom continued. He picked up a piece and handed it to Patrick. He examined the small block of horn and passed it to his companions. The boys realized that what they had thought was plastic was actually polished horn. "The horn tips protect the ends of the limbs from damage. They're called the nocks. We cut special slots in the nock to hold the bow string. When the bow is done, it is finished in oil and wax to make it waterproof, because sometimes we fight in the rain. The bow string is made from flax, a plant we grow. We wax it too, so it's waterproof. "

"You know, Patrick," Mike said. "There's a lot to learn and it will take a long time. Maybe one of us should learn to be a bowyer. Another should learn to be a fletcher, and the other a smith."

"Makes sense," Patrick agreed. "Your father's a woodworker," he said to Mike. "You already know more about wood than Nick or me. You be the bowyer."

"It does make sense for you to each learn a different trade," Tom added. "John," he called to another bowyer. "Can you put

Mike here to work while I take Patrick to the fletcher shed, and Nick to the smith's forge? First, get them leather work aprons to protect their clothes."

Patrick learned to split a short log into thin, straight strips of wood. "This tree is called ash," the fletcher told him. "It's strong and flexible. It's also heavy. A heavy arrow hits with more power. We use lighter woods like willow to make arrows for the boys to use in the butts. Only ash makes a good war arrow."

The fletcher showed Patrick how to round the thin length of wood. Then, he took a wooden hammer and drove the piece through a hole in an iron plate. This made a perfectly straight and round arrow shaft. Next, the fletcher showed Patrick how to cut the nock in the end where the arrow fit over the bow string.

The fletcher took goose feathers and cut them into short pieces. He glued them to the end of the arrow just ahead of the nock. "The feathers make the arrow travel in a straight line," the fletcher said.

'Just like the fins on a rocket,' Patrick thought to himself.

Patrick learned how to attach the hollow end of the steel arrowhead to the shaft. When the arrow was done, it was added to a bundle of arrows. The completed bundle was wrapped in leather. Then, it was packed into a wooden barrel with other bundles of arrows to be sent to the army.

Nick was excited to be in the smith's shop. The smith made arrowheads and this was the kind of work Nick liked. The smith heated steel rods until they were white hot. He did this in a charcoal fire burning in a special furnace called a forge. A type of pump called a bellows blew air into the bottom of the fire to make it burn as hot as possible.

When the steel glowed white hot, the smith took it out of the fire with a pair of iron tongs. The heat made the steel soft so the smith could change its shape by beating on it with a hammer. He made an arrowhead that looked like a long, four-sided spike. "This is called a bodkin point," the smith told Nick. "It's shaped like a nail that carpenters use."

Next, the smith showed Nick how to make the steel bodkin harder than iron. He heated it until it glowed red and quickly stuck it in water. It hissed and sizzled. "This is called quenching," the smith said. Next, he heated the arrow head only until it turned yellow. Then, he quenched the head again. "This is called tempering. Now, the arrowhead is harder than the armor the Frenchies wear," he said. "Its small pointed end will punch a hole through a knight's armor. If the bodkin doesn't kill the knight it will hurt him so badly he cannot fight. A bodkin is a frightening weapon. Nothing can stop it."

Nick tried making a bodkin. Soon, he was turning out an arrowhead every five minutes. "Very good," the smith told Nick. "Some smiths take years to get as fast as you are the first day."

At the end of the day the boys gathered with the bowyers, fletchers, and smiths to hang up their work aprons. "The lads and I are going to the tavern for a mug of ale," Tom said. "Do you want to join us?"

"I think we should see the village and the butts," Patrick said. He didn't think he and his crew would like the taste of ale, and he had learned too much of it makes people talk stupid. The boys couldn't risk saying something that would give them away.

"While you're in Hilton you should stay with me and my family in our cottage," Tom told them. "My home is not as nice as squires are used to, but you'll be well cared for. Mistress Littlefield will serve supper in an hour. Meet me there. The butts are next to the village green. We practice there on Sunday after church. I'll teach you how to shoot a longbow then."

The boys agreed to stay with Tom and his family. Before supper they decided to take a walk together and explore the village. First, Nick stopped at the well to wash his face and hands in a wooden bucket. They were covered with black soot from the charcoal and the smoke. "Making arrowheads is dirty work," he said. "I see you guys stayed pretty clean, but I had more fun."

As the boys passed a row of cottages they glanced inside. These simple homes were all alike. Their walls were made of woven sticks covered with mud, a building method called wattle and daub. The cottages had no windows for light, just small openings without any glass. The homes had thatched roofs. Thatch is straw cut and layered in a special way so it sheds rain. Most houses had two rooms with dirt floors. There was no chimney, only a cooking fire in the middle of one room. The smoke escaped through a hole in the peak of the roof. The inside walls were covered with white plaster that quickly grew black from the smoke from the open fire. The villagers kept their cottages bright by regularly whitening the walls with a type of simple paint called whitewash.

The boys walked to the open field known as the village green. It was where the village folk gathered for ceremonies and festivals. "Don't look now, but I think we're being followed," Mike said to Patrick and Nick. The boys stopped to examine a large, round brick oven with smoke coming out of it. This gave them an opportunity to turn and glance behind.

A group of village girls were following. The girls stopped and giggled when the boys turned. The boys ignored them and continued to the butts. The butts was a narrow strip of grass longer than a football field, with targets placed at different distances from the shooting line. "I guess we'll begin shooting at the closest one," Patrick said. "The others are pretty far away." While the boys looked at the targets the girls caught up with them.

"Are all the boys in Ireland as cute as you?" one asked. "Are Irish girls pretty?"

Mike thought fast. "Irish girls are pretty, but not as pretty as English girls," he said. "Still, I have been promised to a girl named Allie."

"I have been promised to a girl named Lenore," Nick quickly added.

"You did it to me again," Patrick yelled at Mike and Nick as his friends started back to Tom's cottage, leaving him alone with the girls. "I'll get even with you." Mike and Nick laughed as they left Patrick to work his way out of this problem.

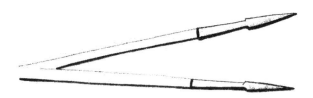

CHAPTER SIX
SUNDAY AT THE BUTTS

Sunday morning the entire village attended Mass at the local church. The boys sat in the small chapel with Tom and his family. It was lunchtime when the people got out. The men walked to the village green while the women went home. On the green the men set up tables that were no more than long, wide boards placed on saw horses. Patrick, Nick, and Mike helped. As the work progressed they understood what was happening. The men were preparing for a big picnic.

Sure enough, the woman began to arrive with food and drink that they spread on the table. Then, the whole village gathered and ate together. The people talked and joked. As soon as they were done with their food, the children began to play. Watching how fast the picnic was prepared, the boys realized the village did this every Sunday. For them, this was a well-practiced routine.

After a while of visiting with neighbors, groups of men began to wander to the butts. Others stayed behind. The women and girls began to clean up and take the leftover food home. The men who remained disassembled the tables and stored them for next week. Then, they joined the other men in the butts. The women and girls came back after returning the food to their homes and sat down on the grass to watch the men.

"The law says every man and boy older than seven years must practice with the longbow two hours every Sunday," Tom explained. "They didn't need to pass a law. We love shooting and we would have practiced anyway. When we're done some of the women and girls will shoot. The entire village loves this sport. It earns us our livelihood, and it amuses us."

Three men advanced to the shooting line with their bows. They all sported leather guards that covered their left wrist and arm. "It's called a bracer," Tom explained. "It protects the archer's arm from the bow string. If the string hits your skin, it stings, and can even draw blood." On their right hands, each man wore a special type of leather glove that only covered his first three fingers. "That protects his hand from the string," Tom told the boys. "It takes a lot of strength to draw a bow. That thin cord cuts into your fingers and can raise blisters."

Mike knew the three archers. They were bowyers and he worked with them. "We shoot as teams," Tom explained. "The bowyers, the fletchers, and the smiths. A little competition adds to the fun. When our wives aren't watching sometimes we'll even bet a pint of ale. It's not much, just enough to make the match interesting. The losers will buy for the winners tomorrow after work."

Each man stuck three arrows into the ground in front of him and put a fourth arrow onto his bow. The three men drew their bows and released their arrows at the first target. The winged missiles made a whizzing sound as they flew down the butts.

"Strange sound," Patrick said.

"That's the sound of arrows going away," Tom said. "These are aimed shots. When an aimed shot is coming at you, you do not hear it. In battle, the archers don't use aimed shots unless the enemy is close. That is a death sentence. No one targeted by an English archer survives at that range. When the other army is far away, we shoot long, high shots called volleys. Those pour down out of the sky on the enemy. When thousands of archers shoot at once the sound is terrifying. The arrows sound like a swarm of angry bees. The arrows create a great, dark cloud and then, a deadly rain falls from the sky.

"The first shot is only 25 yards," Tom said, pointing at the butts. The boys knew that was almost half way across a football field, but it seemed like a long way to them. All the arrows hit the target in the center. "The next one is 50 yards," Tom said. Again, all three arrows hit the center. One was close to the edge of the circle, near the first ring. "Look lively, John," Tom called to the archer.

The next shot was 75 yards. Only one arrow hit the center of the target, but the other two were in the first ring. "Well shot, lads," Tom called to his team.

Finally, Team Bowyer shot at the 100 yard targets. "This is exactly the length of a football field," Patrick whispered to Mike and Nick. "From here that target looks like little more than a dot."

The bowyers took their shots. All of the arrows hit the target, but none was a bull's eye. Tom added up the team's points and called their score to them.

The fletchers shot next. They did even better than the bowyers and were soon ahead in the match. The smiths shot last. As they began, an afternoon breeze came up and created a problem for the archers. The wind could push their shots off their mark. Before shooting each put his finger in his mouth, wet it, and held it in the air. "His finger feels cooler on the breeze side," Tom explained. "He will know which way the air is moving and compensate by shooting a little more in that direction. He will count on the breeze to push his arrow back toward the target." The smiths did well, but the breeze kept shifting and driving arrows slightly off the center. "Too bad, lads," Tom called to them. "You shot bravely."

After the men had shot, the village boys took their turn. Like their fathers, each walked onto the butts carrying his bow and four arrows. Each stuck three arrows into the ground in front of him. The smaller boys had smaller bows and shorter arrows. Patrick,

Nick, and Mike were amazed at how well even the young kids in Hilton could shoot. The men helped the youngest boys and gave them lessons, but let the older boys practice on their own.

"Your turn, my young squires," Tom said to Patrick. The boys put on their leather bracers and gloves. They stepped to the shooting line and stuck their spare arrows into the ground. Each pulled the string on his bow, and sighting down the arrow, pointed it right at the center of the 25-yard target. They let the arrows fly. Not one of the arrows hit the target. In fact, not one even reached it. Their arrows all landed in the dirt well in front of the mark. The villagers all laughed.

Tom stepped up to help the boys. "You aimed your arrows at the target," he said. "The arrow falls as it flies. Aim above the target like you were going to shoot over it. When the arrow falls, it falls into the target. Don't sight along the arrow. Look at the target with your eye, but shoot a bit above it. Try again."

This time Patrick and Nick hit the target. Mike missed, but at least his arrow went far enough. "Well shot," Tom said. "Try again." This time all three hit the target. Patrick even put his arrow in the first ring. "Good," Tom said. "Try again."

The boys shot over and over, only stopping because their arms got tired. "You need to strengthen your muscles," Tom said. "An archer in the army is able to make 20 aimed shots a minute."

"That's one every three seconds," Nick said. "My arms would fall off first."

At the end of the picnic some women and girls took turns shooting in the butts. They were not as good as the men. Still, they were a lot better than the Irish squires. "We need to come to the butts every day after work to practice," Patrick said to Tom.

As the sun was setting Patrick, Mike, and Nick strolled through the village accompanying Tom to his home. The man was quiet and seemed to have something on his mind. "That was fun," Tom said at last. "Today, we shot arrows for sport. Soon, I fear we will be shooting them in anger. Our new king Hal should also be the king of France. He has a good claim to the French throne, but the French want a king from their own people. Englishmen will probably have to fight for King Hal. If we do, he will take an army to France.

"We fight the Frenchies a lot. In fact, I don't remember a time when we weren't at war with them. My father and his father couldn't remember a time of peace. When English archers go to France, a lot of us do not come back. We kill Frenchies by the hundreds, but they always kill some of us. It's not good.

"King Hal pays his archers well. If he invades France I will probably go. So will other men from the village. Mistress Littlefield will not be happy, but I cannot pass up the money. A soldier's pay will take good care of my family should anything happen to me. Still, I'm worried and afraid.

"When you go back to Ireland and you become knights, remember the men who go to war with you. Take good care of them. They have families. They have feelings. They have lives."

Tom became quiet again. On their way home the group passed the small, round brick building with smoke coming out of it. "What is that building?" Mike asked.

"It's a charcoal kiln," Tom said. "The smiths need charcoal for their forges. It burns hotter and more evenly than wood. The man who runs the kiln is called a collier. He's making a load of charcoal right now. That is why his kiln is smoking."

Tom turned to continue the walk back to the cottage. "Young squires, you have learned what you need. You can teach your lord's men how to make and use the longbow. Will you be leaving us tomorrow?"

"You and the other craftsmen have been very kind to us," Patrick replied. "You took time from your work to teach us. We would like to stay another week with you. With our help, maybe we can catch you back up on your work. Maybe we can even help you get ahead. I suggest we leave next Monday. We'll practice with the longbow every day this week. Then, I would like to compete in the butts one more time."

The next afternoon after work the boys walked down to the butts for their daily practice. As they passed the charcoal kiln they noticed the collier had opened it and was taking out the charcoal. "You guys go along," Mike said to Patrick and Nick. "I want to see how this thing works."

The collier was as friendly as everyone else in the village. He explained to Mike the special way he stacked wood in the kiln. "When the kiln is full, I start a fire in the middle of the stack," he explained. "Then, I seal the kiln. Without air, the fire burns very slowly and makes a lot of smoke." The collier picked up a lump of charcoal and showed it to Mike. "This is ready for the smith," he said. Mike thanked the collier and asked if he could take the piece with him.

At the butts Nick and Patrick were already shooting. Some village children had come to watch them. Today, Mike was more interested in the charcoal. It had started out as wood, but now was lightweight and he could crumble it in his hand. He pressed some between two rocks and found it turned into a fine black powder. It got on his hands and he had to wipe the soot on the grass before he took his turn shooting.

The next Sunday, the boys assumed their places in the butts with the village men. Mike shot with the bowyers, Patrick with the fletchers, and Nick with the smiths. During the week they had practiced enough so that at 25 and 50 yards they all hit the bull's eye with aimed shots. At 75 and 100 yards they each hit the target, but didn't get close enough to the center to help their teams. The fletchers won again this week.

The next day, the boys walked to the work sheds with Tom and said goodbye to the craftsmen. "Maybe someday you Irish will march with King Hal," Tom said as they all shook hands. "Maybe we will shoot side-by-side, like we do with the Welsh archers. That will really give the Frenchies something to be afraid of."

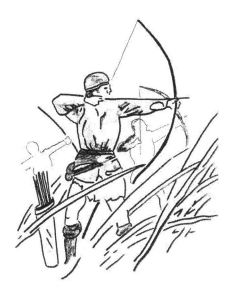

CHAPTER SEVEN
AGINCOURT

The boys climbed into the CT 9225 and Patrick programmed in the sequence for the Battle of Agincourt. The boys arrived at the site of the battle and opened the door to discover a dirt field. After harvesting his crops, the farmer had plowed his field to prepare the land for spring planting. The furrows made the ground look like brown corduroy.

It was a day in late October and it was late in the afternoon. It was also raining. The field was covered with puddles of standing water, telling the boys it had been raining for days and the ground was saturated. The air was damp and chilly.

There was no one around. The three time travelers were alone on the deserted field. "Maybe we got here too early," Mike said. "We would know if we had arrived too late. There would be signs of a recent battle. Battlefields are always a mess."

The plowed area was a long strip of land with woods on both sides. There wouldn't be a lot of space for fighting on such a narrow patch of ground. "It looks sorta like a fairway on a golf course, except it's dirt not grass," Mike said.

"Quiet," Nick insisted. A low rumbling noise was coming from a distance. As the boys listened it grew louder. It was not a single sound like that made by a train or a jet. It was a combination of many noises – a din. There were voices. There was stomping. There was rattling, clanking, jingling, and creaking. It took a while but the source of the noise finally appeared. At the other end of the long strip of ground a group of knights on horseback came into view.

The sight made the boys gasp. They had read about knights and seen them in movies, but these were real, and they were more exciting than the boys could have imagined. The knights carried shields with different, brightly-colored emblems on them. Their polished amour gleamed, even though it was a cloudy day. The horses were covered in colored cloth, decorated with more emblems.

The group of knights stopped at the end of the field and waited. More knights arrived and joined the first group. Still more knights came into view, and then more. The crowd of knights continued to grow. At last, a small cluster of armored men on horseback moved slightly forward of the others and examined the field. They appeared to be talking about the ground and how to best fight on it. The boys guessed these knights were in charge of the army that was continually growing behind them.

More knights streamed into view. Then, even more. In time, the boys could no longer see the rear of the army, there were so many. They could only hear the noise made by those still arriving. The scene changed. Knights on foot began to march onto the field. The boys could see them clearly, as they placed themselves in front of the knights on horses, rather than behind. The line of foot soldiers too flowed onto the field like a continuously growing snake.

It took a long time, but eventually, the procession of armored men on foot ended. The scene was not over. Next, a line of wagons came into view and assembled behind the army. That line too just kept coming, and coming, and coming.

The sight at the other end of the field was unbelievable. It was beautiful and it was frightening. The colors, the banners, the shields, the gleaming armor took the boys' breath away. The very size of the army awed them. There were thousands and thousands of knights arrayed at the other end of the plowed ground. It was like everyone in a football stadium had gotten out of their seats and gone onto the field at once. It was a huge crowd of men in armor making an enormous racket.

"Look," Patrick said pointing in the other direction. Another group of men was slowly approaching the near end of the field from the opposite direction. This had to be the English, and unaware, they were walking right into the enemy. The two forces would soon be face-to-face. The French army was beautiful and thrilling. On the other hand, the crowd of English could hardly be called an army. They presented a miserable sight. Rather than maintain ranks, the men plodded slowly in clusters, hunched over. It was obvious, even from a distance they were hungry, sick, and cold. The horses that pulled the wagons behind the army looked as bad as the men. The boys wondered if this sorry group would have enough strength to make it to the battle, never mind to fight.

The first soldiers of the English front guard arrived at the near end of the field, not far from the cloaked boys. The Englishmen were shocked to discover the other army blocking their way. They scanned the walls of woods on both sides of the field. They were hemmed in. They gaped at the huge sea of color and gleaming armor at the other end. Some of the men crossed themselves and dropped to their knees to pray. One called to an approaching group of men on skinny, hungry horses. The men on horseback spurred their starving nags to join the front guard, and like their comrades, they stared down the long field. "One of those guys must be Henry," Mike said. "I'll bet he's the big guy in the middle on the white horse. Do you know he's six feet three inches tall?"

King Henry spoke with the other horsemen and gestured down the field as they conversed. It was obvious they were discussing what to do. They knew they were in a trap and there was nowhere else to go. Meanwhile, the sick, tired men of their army began to straggle in and gathered in a large crowd behind their king. They too stared down the field and they all looked worried. The army at the other end was many times bigger than theirs. They could see that army was healthy, well-fed, and ready to fight. It would be an uneven match.

Most of the men that clustered on the field with King Hal didn't wear armor. Instead, they wore a hooded, green coat that reached to their knees. Each man had pulled his hood over his head to protect against the rain. Each man had a large leather belt around the middle of his coat. Some carried a knife in the belt. A few had a sword. All these men in green carried something long and wrapped in a shiny cloth. Having worked at Hilton, the boys knew the cloth had been treated with some coating to make it waterproof. Over his shoulder, each man also had a leather tube with a cover to keep out the rain.

The boys recognized the archers and knew what they carried. They had removed the strings from their bows and wrapped them in an oiled cloth to keep them dry. The covered leather tubes were quivers. Each contained about a dozen arrows, just in case of a surprise fight. The bulk of the arrows were stored in barrels carried on the wagons.

The day was ending as the last of the English army arrived. There was no sunset. The day was so dank and gloomy, the sky just got slowly darker. Nick watched groups of archers straggle slowly by when he spotted one he knew. "Tom. Tom Littlefield," he yelled.

Tom looked up and saw the boys. "My young squires," he said with a happy smile. "What are you doing here?"

"We were sent to find King Henry," Patrick said. "Our lord's archers are not ready for battle yet. Still, he wants us to see how the English archers fight and report back to him."

"I'm afraid this will not be our most glorious battle," Tom said sadly. "The lads are all hungry. They're sick. We're no match for the Frenchies. It's too late in the day for them to attack us now. They'll wait until tomorrow. Then, they'll cut us to ribbons.

"Come. Help us set up camp," Tom asked the boys. "We meet our deaths tomorrow, but we still have lots of work to do. We won't go down without giving the Frenchies a good fight." In the growing darkness some archers began to set up tents and gather wood for campfires. Others went into the woods and began to cut small, straight trees. They hacked off all the limbs and piled the long poles on the field.

When it was too dark to work any longer the archers gathered around their campfires and ate supper. It wasn't much. "We have little food left," Tom told the boys. "We've been marching and fighting since August." He invited the boys to share their meal, but they thanked him and said it was more important that the archers eat. They would need their strength in the morning. In reality, the boys were not hungry. They were out of their own sequences and due to the experience of time they did not require food.

A dog began to bark. It was a loud persistent bark that meant business. "It's Frenchie spies," Tom said. Men picked up their weapons and ran toward the dog. "Their spies are trying to sneak into our camp. They want to capture some Englishmen to bring back for questioning. That way, they will find out how strong we are and what we plan to do. That's why we bring our dogs with us. They protect our camp."

"That's unfair, sending spies," Nick said in disgust.

"We're doing the same thing," Tom said without any concern. "Our spies are in the French camp right now. That's what you do in war. You find out as much as you can about the other side. That's how King Hal will decide what to do tomorrow. He'll question the French prisoners and find out what they know."

A small group of archers quietly rose and walked away together. A while later, the archers returned and others got up to leave, going in the same direction as the first group. "What are they doing?" Patrick asked.

"They're going to confession," Tom said. "We know we're going to die tomorrow. Our priests are hearing our confessions and forgiving our sins. We don't want to die with sins on our souls. We want to go up to Heaven, not down to Hell. We'll let the Frenchies go down there."

Tom reached under a cloth and carefully pulled out a large object. "This was John's citole," he said holding up an instrument that looked like a guitar. "You remember John from the village. He was a bowyer like me. He died of the flux while we were marching. He just lay down by the road and gave up the ghost. He asked me to return this to his wife to remember him by. I promised him I'd bring it back to Hilton, but I don't think I'm going to make it either."

Mike recognized the citole as an ancient guitar. "I think I can play that," he said. Tom passed Mike the instrument. Mike took a minute to tune it. Then, he strummed several chords. "Yeah," he said. "I can play this." Mike began a sad tune made famous by Elvis Presley, *Love Me Tender*. He didn't think the words to the song would translate well, so before singing he turned off his translator helmet. The archers heard Mike singing in modern English. They didn't understand the words because they spoke Middle English. They thought Mike was singing in Gaelic, the Irish language.

Archers gathered from nearby campfires to listen. Mike wished he knew some songs the men could sing, but he didn't. Instead, he played sad tunes from his own time. He even played some he had written. Menlo played with a dog friend named Angus that only had three legs. Mike had written a sad song about him. While they listened to the music the archers stared into the fire. Each was lost in private thoughts about the next morning.

Mike played and sang until most of the archers had fallen asleep. Then, he offered the citole back to Tom. "You keep it," Tom said. "Maybe you will escape and you can give it back to John's wife. Tomorrow, if the French capture you, tell them you are nobles. They will not kill you. They will hold you for ransom and make your lord buy you back. That will not happen to the archers. They are angry with us because we don't fight by the rules of chivalry. We are common folk and we kill noblemen. They will kill us out of revenge. I would be happy to go home without my fingers. They can cut those off if they want, but I think I will be killed instead."

As the boys settled in to sleep Nick said, "It's so weird. We know what's gonna happen tomorrow, but we can't tell them. If we could tell them the will win, they would all sleep better."

"Time travel messes with your mind," Mike replied.

There was no sunrise. A growing, gloomy light slowly revealed the landscape through a thin fog. The morning was just as drizzly as the day before, and the woods were still soaked. The low spots in the field were now pools of standing water, larger than the puddles from the evening before. The English army woke and went to work preparing for the battle. Henry assembled his knights at his end of the field, facing the French. It was a pitifully small group. He had few knights on horseback. Most would fight on foot. "Knights without a horse are called men at arms," Tom told the boys. "Men at arms are skilled with the sword. They move their weapon so quickly you can barely see it. The French have so many and we have so few."

King Henry placed his archers on the sides of the field, so they formed a letter V. The open end of this formation faced the French.

Henry gathered his small group of men at arms and knights at the point of the V. This way, his army formed a funnel. To get to the men at arms at the bottom of the funnel, the French would have to pass between the archers and endure their deadly rain.

While the army was getting into formation, runners brought bundles of arrows from the wagons to the archers. The archers opened the bundles and stuck the arrows in the ground in front of them. As soon as an arrow left the bow, the archer could pluck another from the ground. It would be fitted and the bow drawn again. There would be only seconds between volleys. Patrick wondered if any of the bundles were the arrows he had made at Hilton.

The archers continued to prepare. Some used axes to chop sharp points on the ends of the young trees they had cut the night before. Others dug rows of holes in front of their position. They buried the ends of the trees at an angle with the pointed ends out, facing away from them. "These are called palings," Tom explained. "The sharp points will keep the knights on horses at bay. The horses can't get through without being stabbed by the palings. I wish our simple fortifications could stop the men at arms. They will get through and they will be the ones to kill the archers. We have some knives and swords, but no armor. When they reach us we will be hacked to pieces."

The archers watched as the French stirred and slowly prepared for the battle. They didn't seem to be in any hurry. They could afford to be casual about the day ahead. They had the English army trapped. The two armies were so close King Hal's archers could see the enemy clearly. Some French knights were putting money into a blanket. The archers could hear them talking, but they didn't understand the foreign language. Even though the knights were speaking an old version of French, Mike understood some of it. "They're making bets," he told Patrick and Nick. "They're betting who will capture the king and who will kill the most English. They're arguing about who should have the right to lead the charge."

The knights employed men called grooms to take care of the horses. In preparation for the charge the grooms limbered up the animals by walking them in the freshly plowed field between the English and the French. "Are they crazy?" Tom asked out loud. "They're making a big puddle of mud right in front of their army."

A runner approached Tom and spoke with him. "Word just came down from the rear," Tom told the other archers. "A second French army is coming up behind us. We are in a trap that will soon spring shut. If we are to live through this day, we will have to fight our way through this field."

King Henry knew he had little time before the second army arrived. Since the French were in no hurry to start the fight, he would. He ordered his small number of knights on horseback to charge. They did and the French answered the challenge. The French men at arms started running up the field followed by the knights on horses. The French army quickly ran into a problem. The long line of attacking men was wider than the field. The woods on both sides forced the ends of the line to squeeze toward the middle. Soon, more men were charging than could fit on the narrow stretch of land. The men at arms bumped into each other and into the horses.

Another problem popped up. The French ran into the mud where the grooms had warmed up the horses. Men at arms in heavy armor could barely move in the sloppy mess. Horses with heavily armored knights had trouble lifting their legs. King Henry saw his chance. He ordered his archers to fire on the French army stuck in the mud. The result was terrifying. The boys watched a cloud of thousands of arrows fly skyward, buzzing like a huge swarm of angry bees. Then, they began to fall out of the sky.

The horrible killing rain hit both men and horses. The lucky men were killed outright. However, many more had arrows in their necks, arms and bodies. Knights on horseback were hit. Horses had arrows in their necks, their backs, their legs. They whinnied in pain. Some horses fell, landing on their riders, or crushing nearby men at arms that were stuck in the mud. Others animals reared and ran about blindly. They stomped and crushed even more men at arms.

The archers sent in another deadly swarm. They plucked arrows from the ground in front of them and in seconds sent off another cloud, then another, and another. The men at the rear of the French army had not encountered the arrows. They were eager for their chance at glory and tried to push onto the field. There, they ran into the men that were stuck in the mud. They ran into the wounded; they ran into the dead. They too became trapped in the mud as storms of arrows began to fall on them.

Patrick, Nick, and Mike watched from behind the archers. They could not believe what they witnessed. In front of them, men were dying by the hundreds. The screaming of men and horses was mixed with the yells of the archers and the whizzing of the arrows. More and more French knights and men at arms fell. More and more were crushed or trampled by charging, screaming horses, blind with pain. Men at arms who had fallen were pushed into the mud by the men on top of them, and drowned. The chaos was unbelievable. The beautiful French army with its gleaming armor and colored banners became a sea of noise, mud, and blood.

The archers realized the French army was stuck and helpless, and this was their chance to take revenge on the men at arms who would have hacked them apart. They grabbed the shovels, picks, and axes they had used to make and set the palings. They charged down the field and fell on the French, beating them with their tools. Even more knights and men at arms were killed this way. As Patrick looked at the mess of dead men and horses, and the mud stained red with blood he muttered, "I thought this was a glorious victory. If this is what glory looks like, I don't like it."

In time, the field grew less noisy. The wounded French continued to scream in pain, but they slowly bled to death. Every minute there were fewer and fewer of them alive, and dead men make no sound. The English disarmed the French knights who were lucky enough to still be standing and took them back as prisoners. When the prisoners were all gathered, the English set about finding their own dead and wounded. The boys spotted a group of men from Hilton carrying a body and they ran up to them. In shock, they realized the corpse was Tom. He had been stabbed in the chest.

"Oh, Tom. Tom. Tom," Patrick cried. The boys all took hold of Tom's sleeve as tears flowed down their cheeks. They helped carry Tom's body back to their camp where a priest came by and blessed their friend. The men from Hilton found shovels and dug a grave near the woods. They wrapped Tom in his blanket and lowered him into the grave. One of the fletchers prayed. The others told stories about Tom, stories that revealed him to be a funny, generous, and loyal friend. The boys helped shovel the dirt into the grave.

"I've seen enough," Mike said to his two companions. "I want to go back."

"We have to return to Ireland," Patrick told the men from Hilton. "On the way, we'll give John's wife his citole. We'll visit Tom's wife and tell her that he died a hero."

"We need to find a sequence and frame about a month from now," Mike said. "We can't just show up in Hilton and tell people about a battle that happened this morning. News doesn't travel that fast in 1415." Patrick found an appropriate sequence in the directory and took the CT 9225 to it. Then, he flew to Hilton. He landed in a wood and the boys walked into the village where they visited John's and Tom's families. Their wives and children cried. The boys cried with them.

On the way back to the CT 9225 the boys made a final tour around the village. They thought about the good times they had had with the people from Hilton. They thought about the pain and sorrow they had brought here from a faraway battlefield. They thought about the pain and sorrow that was happening in hundreds of homes in England and in France. Whether they lived in cottages or castles, lots of women and children were crying all because Henry wasn't satisfied to be king of England.

CHAPTER EIGHT
THE VISITOR

"I have to talk to Rabbi Cohen when we get back," Mike said. "I need his advice. He helped me when I wanted to stop Allie from going on that mission to Carthage. He helped me and Allie when we got back from Nicopolis."

The boys met Rabbi Cohen in his office and recounted their experiences at Agincourt and their final visit to Hilton. "I know Tom was dead for almost six hundred years before we were even born," Mike said. "Why should his death bother us so much? Why did we all cry for Tom? Why did we all cry with his wife and children? Why do we care what happened to him?"

"Remember what Dr. Newcomb taught you," Rabbi Cohen answered. "Time travel messes with your mind. Right now, you're having a bad case of it." The rabbi paused for a moment and then expressed another thought. "You know everything in this universe comes to an end. I can only think of a couple of things that last forever, love and friendship. All of us will die. When we do leave this life we go out the same way we came in, with nothing. We only take out of this life the kindness we have given to others and the kindness they have given us. It doesn't matter when in time they were our friends and when they were kind to us. It still lasts forever. Tom was your friend and he was good to you. That friendship will live forever. You'll take his kindness with you when you leave this life, just as I'm sure he took your kindness with him.

"Your tears are a good sign," Rabbi Cohen continued. "It means you have empathy. Empathy is the ability to feel what other people are feeling. Empathy is a sign of a truly good person. I'm glad you cried. It reassures me that Dr. Newcomb and I have been right about you. We have always thought you to be special people. You love your friends, and you care about them. You're loyal. Don't ever lose those qualities."

The boys returned to their apartment. The rabbi's remarks had made them feel only slightly better. They still hurt. Allie announced to them that Jen was due back that afternoon and was going to move in with her. They would be roommates again. Allie and the boys decided to have a barbeque by the pool to welcome Jen back. Nick invited Lenore to join them.

Jen arrived just before suppertime. Everyone hugged everyone else. They had not been together since the boys had rescued the lost crew. Mike introduced Menlo. He sniffed Jen's leg and then let her pat him. Soon, Jen was hugging him and getting kisses in return. She giggled as his big, rough tongue tickled her cheek.

Jen had heard about Lenore and the help she had given Nick, but had not yet met her. "I know you've been working with Nick," Jen said to Lenore. "That's the best recommendation you can get. You'll be graduating in a couple of weeks and every pilot without an engineer is going to request you be assigned to his or her crew. Do you mind if I cut to the head of the line? Now that Bashir is working at the Institute lab full time I need an engineer for the Auckland."

"I would love to serve on the Auckland," Lenore responded with enthusiasm. "That way, I would get to work with you and Allie all the time."

"I'll inform the Institute tomorrow that you're my new engineer," Jen said. "Welcome aboard. If Allie agrees, I think it would be real nice if you moved in with us after graduation. There's enough room for three of us in this apartment."

After supper Jen and Allie gathered the dirty dishes and went back to the boys' apartment to serve dessert. As they walked in the door the two girls were startled to find a strange man sitting on the couch. The man stood and the girls screamed. They dropped the dishes.

Patrick and Menlo heard the commotion. Patrick placed his hands on the fence and vaulted over it. Menlo had to run around the fence, but was faster and ended up right behind Patrick. The muscular pilot took the stairs two at a time and burst into the apartment behind the girls, Menlo on his heels. Seeing the stranger, Patrick jumped in front of the girls and put himself in a defensive Tai-Kwon-Do stance. Menlo placed himself beside Patrick and bared his teeth. His hackles, the hair that runs down the center of his back, stood on end. Patrick yelled a challenge. Menlo's ears laid back and he growled menacingly.

The poor stranger was terrified. "I'm sorry. I didn't mean to scare you," he said, trembling and looking back and forth at the martial artist and the threatening dog. "I'm just looking for Patrick Weaver." The man had long hair and a beard. His clothes were strange. They reminded Patrick of the hand sewn, natural fabrics the boys had seen in Hilton. He had a vest with fringe on it and some beads around his neck.

"Why do you want him?" Patrick asked, still ready to put the man on the floor if he acted dangerously. At that moment, Nick, Lenore, and Mike arrived.

"I need him and his team to help me," the man answered. "To help us."

"Who are you?" Patrick demanded.

"My name is Charlie Newcomb," the man said.

"Are you kidding?" Mike asked. "Is this a joke?"

"No," the man answered. "That is really my name."

"Are you related to Dr. Newcomb?" Mike asked suspiciously.

"Yes," the man said. "Dr. Newcomb is my fifth great-grandfather. That's how I knew about Patrick Weaver and his team and why I came here to find them."

It took a second, but the implications finally dawned on Mike. "Are you telling us you're from the future?"

"Yes," Charlie answered. "I came here in a time craft. My family has always told stories about Patrick Weaver and his team. Dr. Newcomb wrote about them in his diary. We still have that diary. He wrote that the team was innovative and courageous. He wrote that they could do things other people could not. He was very proud of them. Do you know where I can find them?"

"I'm Patrick Weaver," Patrick said. He relaxed from his Ti-Kwon-Do stance. "This is Nick Pope and Mike Castleton. This is Jen Canfield, Lenore Smith, and Allie Tymoshenko. They're another time crew. We work together a lot."

"I have found you," Charlie said with relief. "I have found you. Please help us."

"Let's sit down," Mike suggested. "If you want us to help you, you need to tell us what the problem is." Everyone took a seat. Menlo curled up at Jen's feet, but kept one eye on Charlie.

"My world is under attack," Charlie began. "We don't know a lot about the enemy. We call them Dandelions because they are yellow and they just sprung up like weeds. They kill any human they see. I can't even guess how many people have died so far."

He continued his story. "The first Dandelions showed up about a year ago. They appeared just outside Durham, where we live. Since then, they have taken over the city and the surrounding area. Some people from Durham were able to escape. The rest are all dead.

"The Dandelions have a pattern. They take over an area and hold it. That lasts a while. Then, without warning they push out further. When they do, they kill everyone they see. Then, they stop again for a while. We can't get into the areas they take away from us, so we don't know much about them. We don't know where they come from. We don't know why they kill us. We don't know what they want. We don't know what they're doing in the areas they take over.

"They have a weapon. It shoots a blue ball. If it hits you, you die instantly. You do not even scream. We think the weapon explodes all the cells in the body. A little while after being hit, the body turns into a thick, clear liquid. Rain washes it away. Nothing is left."

"What a great weapon," Mike said sarcastically. "It kills and cleans up after itself. The dictators that committed genocide always had to deal with a major difficulty. It's easy to kill masses of people; getting rid of the bodies is the hard part. It sounds like the Dandelions solved that."

"I found an old book that told me how to use a time craft," Charlie continued. "The Dandelions had already taken the area around the old hangers and the arrival/departure pad. I chose a group of young people with the best math skills. We practiced for weeks getting to a craft and programming this sequence. We ran sprints every day so we were in the best possible physical condition, and as fast as possible.

"We ran by the Dandelion guards and all the way to the pad. They followed and killed a lot of us. We only got to the hanger ahead of them because they are slow. I managed to get into a craft and escape. I'm sure all the others are dead."

"Why didn't one your pilots take a craft back?" Jen asked.

"There are no pilots. We don't time travel anymore," Charlie said. "We haven't done that for a long time. No one knows how anymore. That's why I had to learn to operate a craft. Good thing I found this book." He held up the book to show to the two time crews.

"Hey," Patrick said. "That's one of our old text books."

"Why did you stop time traveling?" Mike asked with surprise.

"We don't find any value in it," Charlie answered. "In our time we explore our minds. We mediate a lot and try to improve ourselves. We believe self-knowledge is the most important knowledge. We are quiet and peaceful. The future is wonderful. Anyway, it *was* wonderful. Now, we are helpless. We don't know how to fight. We don't want to fight, but we don't want to die either. We don't know what to do.

"I remembered my family's stories about you. I came to this time to ask you to rescue us. Please. Come back with me. Help us."

Patrick looked around the room. "Any ethic problems?" he asked Mike.

"I don't think so," Mike said. "Anything we do in the future doesn't change any sequences. That only happens in the past." He thought for a minute. "There is a problem," he said. "We'll come back knowing what happens in the future. We could change things now and cause chaos then. If we go there, we all have to swear we will never tell anyone. We can never do anything that could change the future. This mission will have to be a secret just between us. We can't ask Rabbi Cohen for advice this time."

"You know," he continued. "When I was a cadet I asked Dr. Newcomb if time travelers were visiting this time. He said he assumed they were, but we didn't meet them because they had gotten real good at time travel and they didn't make mistakes. Guess what? They're not visiting. They quit. That's why we've never met them."

"If we take this on," Patrick said, thinking out loud, "it's gonna be a big job. We could use some help. Jen, Lenore, Allie, are you up for it?"

"Sure," Jen said. "I wouldn't miss the chance to work with you guys." Lenore and Allie both nodded. "We can't take the CT 9225 and the Auckland. They can't go beyond their frames of origination. How big is your craft, Charlie? Did time craft ever get bigger? Did anyone ever find a way to move more weight at once?"

"Nick did," Lenore added. "The CT 9225 has carried almost twice 400 pounds. It may be able to carry even more. Nick doesn't know for sure yet what the new maximum is."

"Lenore and I can add an amplifier to Charlie's craft," Nick said. "Then we could all go together."

"No you don't, Nick," Mike insisted. "That's my last amp. If you take it we all have to save our allowances to buy some new amps. 'Cause the Sirens are going out of business without them."

"Make it so, Mr. LaForge," Patrick said to Nick, imitating the Captain Picard, the Enterprise's commander from *Star Trek The Next Generation.*

"Huh?" Nick asked.

"Never mind," Patrick said shaking his head. "Just do it.

"Mr. Data," he said to Mike, continuing his Captain Picard imitation. "What are the odds of this mission succeeding?"

Mike understood the joke and played along. "The CT 9225's crew working with the Auckland's crew, Captain? According to my neuro processors, 100%," Mike answered.

"Nick has to make the modifications in secret," Patrick said. "We can't let anyone see an extra time craft on the arrival/departure pad. It would raise questions. They would want to know where it came from. Nick, can you do your work in the woods behind Mike's house? No one will see you there." Nick nodded. "Good. Jen, would you pilot Charlie's craft and take Nick and Lenore to the woods in the morning?"

Jen agreed.

"Charlie," Patrick said. "Nick and Lenore will make some alterations to your craft tomorrow. They'll change it so we can all travel into the future together. Meanwhile, you should stay here with us. You can sleep on our couch. We should be able to leave by tomorrow afternoon."

While Mike and Nick made up the couch for Charlie, the girls went to their own apartment. Menlo left with them. "I think I've lost my dog," Mike said.

CHAPTER NINE

NEW DURHAM

Jen landed Charlie's altered time craft behind the crew quarters where it would not be seen and raise suspicions. Nick and Lenore got out and told the others the job was complete. The craft was ready to go. Charlie knew little about time travel. The future had forgotten how frames and sequences work. He was amazed that someone could go into the past, do a complicated job, and return almost immediately.

"We should bring the same gear we would take on any other mission," Patrick said. "Night vision, helmets, extra cloth cloak covers."

"I suggest we take some binoculars," Mike added as he tossed his football and playbook into the craft. "If we can't get into the areas taken over by the Dandelions, we may have to look in from far away. I don't want to get close to those blue light weapons.

We're gonna have to bring Menlo too," he added. "There's no one here to take care of him. Besides, I remember those guard dogs at Agincourt. If we get into a fight, it may be an advantage to have him with us."

"We have to be sure we can handle the weight," Patrick warned. "Jen," he said. "You should pilot. The craft's mental interface is just getting used to you. I would be the third pilot this poor craft has had in the last few hours, and would confuse it."

With everyone on board, Jen checked the weight indicator. "Seven people, our gear, and one dog, 913 pounds." She turned the dial to see if the craft could carry that load. It could. "Wow," she said. "We were always taught that a time craft could never weigh more than 400 pounds. Nick, you're amazing."

Jen programmed the craft for its frame of origination. During the trip through time Mike amused himself by tossing the football back and forth from hand to hand. Allie said, "Charlie, you told us people in the future spend a lot of time meditating. Tell us more about life then. Tell us what we're going to see when we get there. Tell us anything that could help us."

"As I said, we are a quiet and peaceful people," Charlie told the others. "We have no technology. We gave that up long ago. We only do things that help us to learn about ourselves. We work in the morning. Some of us are farmers and grow food. Growing food is really easy, thanks to Dr. MacDonald's discovery. The rest of us make the things we need. We don't use machines. We work by hand. That allows us to think as we work and to know ourselves better. Some of us are potters. Some work with metals. Some make cloth. Others work with wood. We only work with natural materials.

"We have lots of artists, writers, and musicians. These people use art to explore their own minds. Through their work they help the rest of us to learn more about ourselves."

"Will your people fight the Dandelions, if they have to?" Patrick asked.

"We don't want to fight," Charlie answered. "We would rather live in peace with them. Perhaps we and the Dandelions could even learn from each other. We have to find a way to talk to them. It is evil for them to kill us. We think they do it because they misunderstand us. A group of our leaders is going to talk to them and to offer peace."

"What do you want us to do for you?" Nick asked.

"I don't know," Charlie answered with desperation in his voice. "I only have my grandfather's diary and our family stories. Dr. Newcomb wrote that you solved problems, that you fixed things. He wrote you were very clever. I knew I had to find you and I'm hoping you will solve this problem for us. Maybe you could ask the Dandelions to live in peace with us. I just don't know what I want. I'm confused. I want you to help us."

Jen announced they had arrived at the time craft's frame of origination. She circled the craft above a city. More exactly, what used to be a city. Trees, bushes, and weeds had taken over. "Where is this?" she asked.

"That's Durham," Charlie answered.

"It doesn't look like you took good care of it," Lenore said. "It's all overgrown. What happened to the University of New Hampshire? What happened to the Time Institute?"

"Before we were forced out of Durham we still used some of the buildings," Charlie explained. "We didn't need the others anymore. We don't do the things you used to do. We don't study the things you used to. Science, engineering, history, languages, they're not important. They don't help us to know ourselves.

"Don't land in Durham," he warned Jen. "The Dandelions took it over. That's why my friends and I had to run all the way to the old arrival/departure pad and the hanger. We don't know why they wanted UNH. It's not much use anymore.

"Land over there, outside of Durham," he pointed. "That's where we are living, now that we have been pushed out. We created a village that we call New Durham. It's not much, but we are warm and dry. We'll stay there until the next time the Dandelions push out. I hope we can make peace with them before that happens. They can keep UNH. We only want our village and peace."

Jen set the craft down at the edge of the village. "New Durham looks a lot like Hilton," Mike said to Patrick and Nick.

"Where are all the people?" Allie asked. Mike and the others looked at her, puzzled by her question. "Where are all the people?" Allie repeated. "New Durham is a village. In our time Durham was a city. Now, it's deserted and empty. Where are all the people? There should be hundreds of thousands of them, but all that's left is a small village. Charlie where are the missing people? Why are there so few of you?"

"They left," Charlie answered matter-of-factly.

"Where did they go?" Allie pressed. Charlie shrugged his shoulders. "You lost an entire population and you don't know where they went?" Allie said in disbelief.

"They left," Charlie repeated. "Everyone left. It was long ago. No one remembers much about it. They just left. A few stayed behind. We are their children's children."

"Weird," Mike whispered to his friends. "Allie's right. There should be a huge population. Charlie says they left but he doesn't know why. He doesn't know where they went. And he doesn't seem to care."

As Charlie stepped out of the time craft villagers saw him and ran up to him, asking questions. Most of these folks were related to the young people that had run to the time craft hanger with him and they wanted to know what happened to their family members. Charlie was surprised by their questions. He had experienced so much during his visit to the past that to him, the race to the hanger seemed long ago. Time travel was messing with his mind, but for his neighbors, the chase through Durham had just happened. He gave them the bad news. Many put their faces in their hands and cried. Charlie told them the other runners were heroes. They had done their best and they had given their all. They had given their lives.

Charlie led the time crews and Menlo through the village to an open area where a larger group of people had gathered. "What's happening?" Charlie asked a woman he knew.

"The leaders are getting ready to for their peace mission," she answered. "They're going to walk across the field to the edge of Durham. We can see some Dandelions in the distance. They'll try to talk with them. The Dandelions must have leaders and ours will ask to meet with them. They'll explain that we are friendly and mean them no harm. We're sure the Dandelions will want to live in peace once they know that."

"Take me to your leader," Mike muttered to Patrick. Patrick grimaced at the joke. Like Mike, he didn't think this peace mission was a good idea.

A group of older people stepped out of the crowd. There were about 25 of them. They were dressed in colorful, homemade clothes and wore jewelry made by the village artists. They all had long hair. Some of them had beads and flowers woven into their locks. The men had beards.

"Hippies took over the future," Mike muttered in surprise. "Love and peace, man. Kumbaya, flower power, and the Age of Aquarius."

"We're going to Durham," one of the women in the group announced to the crowd. "I've been chosen to speak for us. If the

Dandelions do not understand our language we will use gestures to show them that we come in peace."

The village people accompanied the group of leaders to see them off on their peace mission. The two time crews and Menlo followed along too. The villagers stopped at the edge of the field and watched as the leaders continued toward old Durham. The people, the time crews, and the leaders could see a cluster of four Dandelions in the distance, across the field. However, the Dandelions didn't appear to pay any attention to the large crowd of people, or the approaching leaders. It was like they were not there.

The time crews were curious to see what the Dandelions looked like and studied them through their binoculars. They were strange beings. They were taller than humans. They were also broader than humans, like football players in full pads. They were smooth and all yellow. They had no faces and nothing that looked like a mouth, eyes, or ears. They had no hair. The boys were not sure if they were robots, or if they were wearing an outer shell. They moved more slowly than people do.

Menlo's hackles stood on end. He growled softly as he stared at the Dandelions in the distance. He stared so hard he didn't even blink. His tail stood straight in the air like an upside down J. "I don't think he likes Dandelions," Lenore said.

"I've never seen him like this," Mike added. "Menlo, be good." The dog ignored him and continued to growl.

The Dandelions paid no attention to the group of leaders as they walked across the field. As they got closer the leaders began to call out, "Peace. We come in peace! We want to talk with you. We will not harm you." They held their arms out in front of them with the hands upward. They wanted to show the Dandelions they did not have weapons. It is also the gesture people use to say "Welcome."

Watching through their binoculars, the time teams weren't sure if the Dandelions could hear the delegation from New Durham. The group was getting close to the four yellow figures, but the Dandelions seemed unaware of the humans. The village leaders got even closer, still calling "Peace. We come in peace." The Dandelions continued to stand perfectly still, like mannequins in a store window.

The leaders were almost within touching distance when suddenly, the four Dandelions raised their arms. Through their binoculars the time teams could see each was holding something shaped like a gun. Four blue balls of light flew from the weapons and hit four people. They dropped like stones. There was no sound. There were screams, but those came from the other leaders. They had turned and were trying to run away. Balls of blue light hit each one in the back. As soon as one was hit, he or she dropped on the spot. Four at a time, the whole group of humans was killed while the people from New Durham and the time teams watched in horror. It happened fast. As soon as the last human was dropped, the Dandelions became just like before. They stood as if nothing had happened. They didn't examine the bodies. They didn't look at the people in the distance.

The people of New Durham were in shock. For a couple of seconds, they stood frozen, staring across the field. Then, they started screaming and running back to the village. Only Charlie and a few of his friends stayed with the time teams. They watched the Dandelions for a while and then walked slowly home.

Lenore and Jen were the most upset. "I can't believe they just killed those poor people," Lenore cried. "How could they be that cruel? Those people weren't going to hurt them. Anyone could see that. They did it on purpose." Nick hugged Lenore and she cried on his shoulder. Menlo bumped her hand with his nose to offer his comfort.

"Even when I was a slave, I never saw anything that cruel," Jen said.

"We've seen a lot of people killed," Patrick said to comfort Jen and Lenore. "It's always hard. The first time is the worst, but you never get used to it."

Allie was quiet. Mike asked her if she was okay. "No," she answered. "I'm afraid. I know this feeling. It's fear. It's how I felt when I was at the hospital. It's how I felt every time I thought about Demetrius. He could whip or brand a slave on the face and act like nothing had happened. He was just like those Dandelions. I've just seen evil again, and I'm afraid. Evil does what it wants without ever feeling sorry. This time though, I will stop it. It won't get away from me this time. You, me, the others, we have to stop it."

Mike put his arm around Allie's shoulder. "We will," he said reassuringly. "We will."

Back in the village Charlie went around to the homes calling people to assemble for a meeting. In an open space he stood on a bench so everyone could see him and announced in a loud voice, "I have brought help. I have brought you the people I told you about, the ones my grandfather knew. I have returned with Patrick Weaver and his friends. They are here to help us."

Charlie beckoned to the boys to get up and speak. "Say something, Patrick," Nick said, pushing Patrick towards Charlie and the bench.

"No way," Patrick said. "Mike. You speak. You're better at this stuff than I am. You always talk to the audience when the band is playing."

Mike stepped up on the bench with Charlie. "We all saw what just happened," he said loudly so the crowd could hear. "I think we all learned something important today. The Dandelions do not want peace. They kill humans. You will not be able to make peace with them. You will not be able to live side-by-side with them. They made that clear today. It will be you or them. You have a choice. You can all die as the Dandelions take over. Or, you can fight."

"We can't fight," a man yelled from the crowd. "We're peaceful people."

"Then you will all be dead people," Mike answered soberly.

"We don't know how to fight," a woman called.

"We do," Mike replied. "We will show you how."

"We don't have weapons," another man called. "We don't know how to make them."

"We will teach you," Mike said. "We will teach you how to make weapons. We will teach you how to use them. We will teach you how to fight. You have no choice. You either fight, or this will be the last generation of human beings on the planet Earth."

That worked. People began to argue among themselves. Some were unsure this was the right thing to do. However, others agreed with Mike and they convinced the crowd of villagers.

"The days of peace are over," Mike said. "At least for a while. Peace only means death for you and your children. Fighting may mean death too. However, it is the only chance you have. My friends and I are going to find out more about these Dandelions. Then, we'll draw up a plan. When we're ready, we'll call you together again. We'll tell you what we have learned and what we propose we should do.

"We will not leave you to do this alone. We came here to help. We will fight along with you. We're not from this time, but we are your friends. Friendship is the only thing that lasts forever. All that really matters in this life is the kindness we do for others and the kindness they do for us."

Mike got down and walked back to his friends. "You just made some big promises," Patrick said to him. "I hope you have some ideas. We're not going to beat the Dandelions with cans of tuna, like we did Dr. Morley and his minions."

"I know what we're going to do," Mike said. "At least I hope I do. We need to meet with some of those craftspeople Charlie told us about. We need to find some woodworkers and some metal workers. You, me, Nick, we're going into the longbow business."

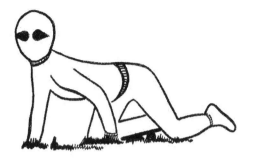

CHAPTER TEN
SPIES

The next day, Charlie Newcomb accompanied the two time crews as they visited with the village wood and metal workers. The boys described to these craftspeople what they had seen and learned in Hilton. They explained the special way that village was organized. Working in that manner, a small group of craftspeople was able to make so many of the longbows and arrows used by the English army.

The wood and metal workers agreed to organize themselves the same way and to make the weapons the village needed to fight the Dandelions. They began to build sheds where they would be able to work together to produce hundreds of bows and many thousands of arrows and bodkin points.

"While they prepare to go into production we need to learn more about the Dandelions," Mike said. "Remember the spies at Agincourt trying to capture soldiers at night so they could be questioned? We need to capture a Dandelion and make it talk."

"What are you thinking?" Patrick asked.

"We sneak across the field under cloak tonight," Mike answered. "With night vision we find a Dandelion standing off by itself. Six of us should be able to capture it." Everyone agreed with the plan.

That night Patrick led six cloaked time travelers across the field. Before they left, Mike put a rope around Menlo's neck and asked Charlie to take care of him. The night vision goggles lit up the field as the crews walked across it. The crews could see everything. However, they couldn't see any Dandelions. Patrick spoke through his head cover microphone to the others. Nothing else in the field, other than his fellow time travelers, could hear him. "Where are they?" he asked. "This is the place where the leaders were killed."

"Could they have gone back to Durham for the night?" Jen asked.

"Maybe they don't post any guards because they don't worry about humans attacking," Allie said.

"Let's not give up right away," Mike argued. "Let's move a little closer toward the city. Getting a captive is too important to quit now."

"We should spread out," Nick suggested. "We can cover more ground." The crews opened more space between themselves. They could see clearly but moved carefully so as to not make any noise.

Lenore noticed a large, dark shadow in front of her. This was not a surprise. Even looking through night vision goggles there were areas with more and less light. She walked straight ahead to pass through the shadow, but to her surprise, she ran into something solid. It was solid and it was big. Unable to see it, she explored it with her hands. She felt arms, and she felt the shadow move. Right away, she knew what it was. She dropped to her knees and began to run away on all fours.

The Dandelion had been surprised too. It pulled out its weapon and began to fire blue balls where it had felt something touch it. The rest of the spies saw the silent blue balls traveling through the darkness. Patrick called, "Everyone. Check in. Who's it firing at?"

Jen, Allie, Mike, and Nick checked in. "It has to be Lenore," Patrick said. "Lenore. Lenore. Where are you?"

"I'm getting out of here as fast as I can," Lenore answered. "I'm on my hands and knees. I don't think it can see me. It's shooting wildly."

"Do you need help?" Nick asked.

"No," Lenore said. "I'm up on my feet now and running."

"Meet at the edge of the field," Patrick said as the six cloaked time travelers ran back towards New Durham.

"Lenore, report," Patrick said as the time crew returned to the village. "What happened?"

"I bumped into a Dandelion" Lenore said. "I didn't see him. All I saw was a shadow. It tried to walk through it and discovered it was solid. I surprised it as much as it surprised me. I figured it would start shooting, so I dropped onto my hands and knees to get below the weapon."

"Why did it look like a shadow?" Jen asked. "Do they cloak, or something?"

"The night vision goggles see heat," Nick explained. "The warmer something is the more light it gives off. Warm looks lighter and cool looks darker. If the Dandelion was just a shadow, I'm guessing it's cold. Our night vision goggles won't see them. They'll look like shadows."

"I don't like trying to capture something I can't see," Patrick said.

"We'll have to try again in daylight," Mike answered. "We're still invisible when cloaked. The problem will be that the other Dandelions may see what's happening to their friend. They'll come to the rescue. We'll have to be really careful. We can't take on a group of them."

"We should wait a couple of days," Allie advised. "They're on edge right now. They'll settle back down eventually, if nothing else happens."

"Agreed," Mike said. "And if we try a daylight capture we had better take some weapons with us, just in case there's a fight."

In a matter of days the wood and metal workers had set up their sheds. When they were ready to go to work Mike taught some woodworkers to make bows. Patrick showed others how to make arrows, and Nick taught the smiths to make bodkin points. The boys explained to the village leather workers what a bracer looked like and they described an archer's glove. Weavers began to twist flax bow strings. Beekeepers brought in wax to protect the bows and strings from rain.

Nick had brought a time craft cloak cover on the mission. Clothing makers cut it into strips to make invisible quivers and cases for the bows. The next time the two crews tried to capture a Dandelion, they would carry weapons with them, but they didn't want those weapons being seen.

Next, the boys set up the butts outside the village. They put targets at 25, 50, 75, and 100 yards. They took the first bows and arrows made by the New Durham bowyers, fletchers, and smiths, and began to train Jen, Lenore, Allie, and Charlie to shoot. The boys taught Charlie and the girls in the same way Tom had taught them. The four practiced several hours every day. The first couple of days their shoulders hurt from pulling the bow. In time, their muscles got stronger, and in a week every arrow hit the center of the target at 25 and 50 yards.

A couple of weeks later, the two crews were ready to try capturing another Dandelion. Mike put the rope around Menlo's neck and asked Charlie to take care of his dog again. At the edge of the field the two crews could see Dandelions on the other side. They were in luck. Some of the Dandelions were standing apart and alone. The crews started across the field fully cloaked.

"Let's try for the one under the tree," Patrick said to the others. "It's farther away from the others, and maybe the tree will give us some cover while we tie it up. We'll circle behind it and all jump it at once."

Patrick watched his companions as they circled behind the Dandelion they had selected to become their captive. The Dandelion didn't move. Patrick hoped that meant the tall, yellow figure could not see the cloaked time travelers sneaking up on it. Still, he worried. He remembered the Dandelions had not paid any attention to the village leaders, until they killed them.

It turned out the Dandelion could not see the cloaked crews and they had no trouble sneaking up on it. When all six were behind their target Patrick whispered, "Now." Nick and the girls jumped onto the Dandelion's back. Mike and Patrick slammed into its legs. The Dandelion fell. However, it was far stronger than they had imagined. It threw the four, unseen attackers off its shoulders, then stood up and reached for its weapon. Seeing what it was about to do, Patrick grabbed its arm and held on while the others escaped. Mike grabbed the other arm. The Dandelion swung its arms wildly while the boys held on for dear life. Meanwhile, the other four time travelers got away.

Finally, the Dandelion threw Mike with such force he rolled across the grass. He got up and ran back to help his friend. The Dandelion flung Patrick off its other arm. He pulled his weapon and began firing in Patrick's direction while Patrick scrambled to get to his feet. The Dandelion couldn't see Patrick, but the others could. They could see the blue balls were getting close.

Mike knew the next shot would find the mark, so he jumped onto the Dandelion's weapon arm. The yellow figure responded by striking its unseen attacker with its free arm, causing Mike to fall to the ground in front of it. The Dandelion couldn't see Mike, but it knew where he was. It pointed its weapon at the spot on the ground right in front of its feet.

Mike watched, knowing he was about to die. It was like everything was in slow motion. The Dandelion lowered its weapon until it was aimed right at him. As he waited for death Mike heard a sound like someone stomping on an aluminum soda can. The Dandelion fell backwards with a longbow arrow sticking out of its chest.

Mike looked up in surprise. Allie stood about 25 yards away with her bow in her hand. She had already pulled out another arrow just in case the first one didn't do the job. She wouldn't need it. The Dandelion was lying on its side and didn't move. The bodkin point had gone in the front and out its back, killing it instantly.

Nick and Lenore ran up to the Dandelion and examined its body. Nick grabbed its head and pulled off a hard, shell-like helmet. He and Lenore were shocked at what was under the helmet and backed up in fear. The others gathered round to see what was inside the suit of armor. It certainly wasn't a robot. The head had yellow eyes with black oval pupils. It had no ears, just small holes in the side of its head. It had nostrils, but no nose. Its tongue was hanging out of its mouth. It was long and forked. It had no hair. Instead, its skin was covered with scales.

"It's a lizard," Patrick said in disgust. "Gross."

"It's reptilian," Mike corrected.

"Look out," Jen warned. Two other Dandelions had spotted their companion on the ground and were walking toward it. The time crews were still invisible, but the Dandelions had surprised them and had gotten too close for comfort.

The crews started to run away. Patrick looked around as he ran. He could see Nick carrying the Dandelion's helmet. "Did somebody get the weapon?" he called to the others. No response. The pilot knew they had left something really important behind.

At that moment Menlo came running across the field going in the direction of old Durham. He had a length of rope hanging from his neck. The cloaked crews could see the rope had been chewed through. Menlo could smell the time crews, but he didn't see them. However, he could see the Dandelions and he was barking at them. Being a Foxhound Menlo bayed. Baying is a long bark that sounds like arooo-rooo-rooo-rooo. Arooo-rooo-rooo-rooo. The Dandelions spotted the dog and pointed their weapons at him. Blue balls flew, but Menlo was moving too fast for them to get a good aim. He ran behind the slow moving Dandelions and with his mouth grabbed the weapon lying on the ground beside the dead one. He tossed the weapon in the air as he ran and caught it again on the fly.

Mike realized Menlo was playing, but was in danger. The dog didn't know what the blue balls were or what they could do to him. He didn't even seem to notice them. Mike knew Menlo would come to him if he could see his master, so he uncloaked. "Menlo, here," he called. Menlo heard the command. He spotted Mike and began to run to him. He wanted Mike to play fetch with his new toy.

The Dandelions saw Mike uncloak as well. One raised his weapon and a blue ball flew fast and silent through the air. For the second time in a matter of minutes, Mike felt time slow down as his life came to an end. The ball flew straight at him, but just before it hit it evaporated like a small cloud. Mike felt stinging and burning all over his body.

He also heard again the sound of a crushing soda can. The two Dandelions fell, both with arrows in the chest. Mike looked and saw his five companions putting more arrows on their bows. "Let's get out of here," Patrick said.

"No," Mike answered. "If we leave these three Dandelions here, they'll be found. The others will know we have a weapon that will kill them. We want to keep that a secret as long as possible.

Let's drag them into the bushes and hide them. There are so many Dandelions in Durham; maybe they won't miss these three.

It took all six time travelers to drag one Dandelion. "They're heavy," Lenore said. The time crews covered the dead Dandelions with brush to make it even harder to find them. Mike broke off the bodkin points and then pulled out the rest of the arrow shafts. "If they do find the bodies, the others won't know what killed them. They'll just have small holes in their armor."

Back in the village the crews sat at a table near the butts with Charlie and some of his friends. "We learned some important information today," Patrick told them. "The Dandelions are not robots. They are reptilian. They wear a yellow armor. Nick and Lenore have examined the helmet and found that the armor isn't very strong. We don't think it's supposed to protect the Dandelions. We think it keeps them warm. Mike says reptiles need heat to stay active, and without heat they shut down. The armor keeps all the heat inside. That's why it's cold on the outside. That's why Lenore thought a Dandelion was a shadow.

"The Dandelions are strong. Mike says all reptiles are strong. However, we know a bodkin arrow will punch right through their armor and we can kill them.

"We got one of their weapons. We don't know a lot about it yet. Nick and Lenore will have to spend more time studying it. We do know one thing; it has a limited range. We know our longbows have a lot longer range. To fight, they have to get closer than we do. That's a real advantage for us."

"Where are the Dandelions from?" Charlie asked. "Why are they here? Did they just come to kill us?"

"We don't know the answers to those questions," Mike said. "I guess the Dandelions are either from another planet, another dimension, or they are time travelers from a very distant future. Perhaps they evolved and took over the earth after humans became extinct.

"We don't know why they're here. We need to go into Durham to get answers to both questions."

"Next, we need your people to start learning to use the longbow," Patrick said to Charlie and his friends. "Humans need to go on the offensive. No more running away."

CHAPTER ELEVEN
BATTLE OF THE FIELD

The New Durham bowyers produced more and more bows. Soon, the time crews began to train the village men, woman, and teenagers to shoot. Every afternoon, instead of meditating, everyone was asked to go to the butts and practice with the longbow.

One afternoon as the villagers shot arrows at the targets, Mike sat under a tree to relax. He studied the playbook the football coach had given him and decided to try some of the plays he was learning. "Hey, Nick," he called. "Run straight away from me and then turn. See if I can throw a football to where you are." Nick ran straight and then turned so he was facing Mike. His path was like the letter J. Mike threw the ball so it hit Nick directly in the chest. All Nick had to do was close his hands and he had made the catch.

"Not bad," Mike said. "Now, run straight, but go a long way. When I yell, look back and see if you can catch the ball. I'll throw it a bit over your head. You'll have to reach up and catch it." Nick went long. Even at a greater distance Mike threw the ball less than a foot over his head. Nick looked back over his shoulder, raised his hands and pulled down the ball. He continued running towards an imaginary end zone.

"Cool," Mike said to himself with satisfaction. "Let's try passing some more," he yelled to Nick."

As Nick ran the ball back to Mike he called to his friend, "Where did you learn to pass like that?"

"I don't know," Mike answered. He felt his right shoulder with his left hand and noticed it was larger and stronger than on the other side of his body. "I wonder where I got all the muscle?" he mused. He nodded as he realized the answer. "Pulling a longbow has strengthened my shoulder and I have a lot more muscle on that side. I guess what helps in archery, helps in football. Go out for another long pass. I want to see how far I can throw this ball."

While Mike was passing to Nick, Jen, Allie, and Lenore walked by on their way to watch the archery.

"What are you guys doing," Jen asked.

"We're practicing some football plays," Mike answered.

"What's football?" Allie asked.

"It's a game that was real popular in our time," Mike replied. "It's played by two teams of eleven players. Our school has a football team and I'm going to try out this summer."

"Teach us how," Lenore said. "We'll play the game with you."

Mike showed the playbook to the girls. He explained where each one should stand and what they would do when he gave the command. "For signals, the A Squared team uses 'Go' and 'Double Go,' " he told them. "Listen for the call. That's what starts the play."

Jen played center with Allie and Lenore as guards. Nick was the End. As they ran plays young people from New Durham began to gather and watch. "What are you doing?" a young man asked.

"We're playing football," Lenore said. "We need another team. Why don't you guys make a team and play with us?"

Soon touch football became an everyday activity. While others practiced archery in the butts, football was played on the village green. The New Durham Longbows always beat the Time Institute Cadets. The reason was simple. The New Durham team had a very big lineman. He was easily able to push the small time travelers, Allie, Jen, and Lenore, out of the way. He always touched Mike before he was able to throw the ball to Nick.

The Time Institute team needed more muscle in its line. The girls found Patrick teaching archery at the butts. "We need you on our team," they instructed him. The girls placed Patrick in the most obvious spot, up against the New Durham player. With Patrick keeping the New Durham lineman out of the back field, scores became more even. However, the Time Institute team still lost every game.

"They're bigger than we are," Mike said. "We have to become more clever. We need to work on our passing game."

"Let's go over the playbook and look for plays that fool the other team," Lenore suggested. "Their speed and size won't help them if they don't know where the ball is."

"Lenore's right," Allie added. "If we keep them guessing who has the ball, Nick has time to get down field." Mike was amused that the three girls had gotten so much into football and had proved to be so competitive. After all, they didn't even play the game in their time. At morning football practice the two crews worked on hand-offs and reverses. Then, Mike practiced his long pass. Nick was so tall and had such long arms, he could catch just about any pass, no matter how far off the mark it was.

In the afternoon the New Durham villagers gathered to watch the two events, the two teams playing football, and the archers practicing in the butts. This gave Mike an idea and he suggested it to Patrick, "Remember in Hilton, they turned every Sunday into a picnic and had contests? Let's do that here. Let's get everyone together for a celebration. We'll hold archery contests. It'll be fun, and we'll find out who the best shots are. In a fight, we may have to depend on them. We can have a football game after the archery."

The next Sunday the entire village gathered at the butts and everyone brought food and drink. They set up long tables so the villagers could eat as much as they wanted. After eating, the boys organized the archery competitions. They gave a red bracer to the very best shots, the archers who could hit the center of the target at 100 yards. Those that could hit the center at 75 yards were given a green bracer. Those who could hit the center at 50 yards got a blue bracer. Those who could only hit the center from 25 yards wore a white bracer.

"This way, we can quickly divide them by skill if we need to," Mike told his companions. "In a fight, we want those who can hit at 100 yards firing first. We have to keep those with white bracers safe in the rear. They can only hit at 25 yards. The Dandelions' weapons kill at 40 yards. The people with white bracers would be dead before they could stop a Dandelion."

A pretty woman in a blue dress and carrying a young child approached Charlie Newcomb. She had long, blond hair with flowers woven in her braids. "Dear, would you hold Charles while I take my turn in the butts?" she asked.

"Of course," Charlie said, giving the woman a kiss and taking the baby. "Heather, meet my friends. This is Mike and Allie, Nick and Lenore, Patrick and Jen. This is my wife, Heather, and my son, Charles." Allie reached out to take the baby from him. She and the other girls started cooing and talking baby talk. Menlo came over to see what this new thing was. When he realized it was a little person, he kissed the baby's face.

"Another Charles Newcomb?" Nick asked.

"There has been one in every generation of my family for as long as we know," Charlie answered. "It seemed right to carry on the tradition."

"We now know four Charles Newcombs," Mike said. "our music teacher at Atlantic Academy, Dr. Newcomb at the Time Institute, you, and your son. We have liked every one of them. I hope there will be lots more Charles Newcombs."

The celebration continued through the afternoon. As it grew late, groups of villagers sat on the grass under trees and rested. They chatted while a few diehards practiced in the butts. Children played with the football and ran around the groups of adults. It looked like a Fourth of July picnic in a small town.

Menlo was asleep beside Jen when he suddenly went on alert. He sniffed the air and cocked his head. He stood up and faced the field. His hackles stood up again. So, did his tail. It curled right over his back. He growled and ran off toward the field and the old city of Durham. No one paid any attention to him.

Menlo reached the edge of the field and began baying as loudly as he could. Aroo-roo-roo-roo. Aroo-roo-roo-roo. Aroo-roo-roo-roo. He ran back and forth across the edge of the field. Aroo-roo-roo-roo. Aroo-roo-roo-roo. Aroo-roo-roo-roo. Finally, Mike investigated what had agitated the dog. "What are you barking at you silly hound?" Mike asked as he walked over to get Menlo.

When he got to the edge of the field he looked across and saw what had upset the dog. It upset Mike too, and made his legs wobble like spaghetti. A long line of Dandelions was marching across the field, stretching from one edge to the other. Mike guessed there were about 300 of them. He had not seen anything like this since Agincourt. The scene was both thrilling and frightening.

He ran back to the village while Menlo continued running back and forth across the edge of the field, baying. "Attack," Mike yelled at the top of his lungs. "It's an attack. Get the archers. They're attacking."

It took a second for the villagers to understand that Mike was raising the alarm. Once they did, they grabbed their bows and quivers and a crowd of archers ran to the field. They villagers stopped in shock when they saw the approaching battle line of Dandelions stretched across the field. "They're pushing out again," Charlie explained. "This is what they did the last time. They come out in a long line and they kill anyone they meet. Then, they stop and hold that new area. It looks like they plan on taking New Durham."

"Not this time," Patrick said. "We've got a surprise for them."

"Patrick," Mike said to his friend. "You and Jen are the only ones who have had leadership training. You two have to take command."

Patrick got that look of resignation that comes over him whenever heavy responsibility lands on his shoulders. A second later he snapped out of it. "Right," he announced. Mike knew Patrick had just risen to the occasion. "Jen," Patrick said. "Will you take command on the left? I'll take the right. Everyone, listen.

They outnumber us three to one. We have to spread out, or they will encircle us. All of you with a red bracer step forward and spread out in a line across the edge of the field. There are not a lot of you and there will be a lot of space between you. Green bracers, form a line behind the reds. Stand between them. Blue bracers, form a line behind the greens. Make sure you have an opening in front of you for a clear shot. White bracers, you are the reserve. Stand behind the blues. You will shoot at close range if they break through. All lines, hold your fire and wait for my command. I will call your color when you are to start shooting." The archers spread out and took their positions by color. They stuck extra arrows in the ground in front of them.

"Mike, I want you to take Allie, Nick, and Lenore with you," Patrick told his friend. "Charlie, get some of your friends. Go along the sides of the field. Remember the archers at Agincourt? We want to make the enemy pass through a funnel. As their line passes by, pick off the Dandelions on the end of the row. After they pass, close in behind them and start shooting from behind. We'll have them in a trap."

Mike and Charlie jogged off in two different directions with their groups. They hunched down and trotted along the sides of the field to get into position. Then, they waited for the long line of Dandelions to pass in front of them. Meanwhile, Patrick and Jen placed themselves out in front of the line of archers. Patrick and Jen were afraid, but they knew everyone else was too. They had been taught at the Time Institute that people will follow a leader willing to face the same danger. "Lead from the front," their teacher had said. Standing in front of the line, everyone could see Jen and Patrick had placed themselves in danger. They realized that their leaders, strangers from another time, were risking death for people they had only recently met. Encouraged by Patrick and Jen, the villagers would risk death too.

The two pilots watched the slow line of Dandelions advancing straight at them. As they paced back and forth in front of the firing line they spoke calmly to their archers. "Steady. Don't panic. Steady. Hold fast. Don't shoot until my command. They are not going to take our village. This is as far as they go. From now on, we take land back from the Dandelions. They're *never* gonna take any more from us."

As the yellow line began to pass Mike and his group, the Fixer S/O waved a signal to Charlie standing on the other side of the field. Both sides started shooting arrows and Dandelions on the ends of the line began to fall. The other Dandelions didn't seem to notice. The line kept moving steadily forward.

The villagers cheered as they saw the line shrink. Charlie's and Mike's groups had dropped 15 to 20 Dandelions on each end. As the line walked by them, the two groups moved in behind and began shooting even more Dandelions in the back. As the yellow line marched forward, the groups followed, picking off more and more of the attackers. The green, grassy field was scattered with yellow bodies, resembling in a macabre way, real dandelions.

Lenore pulled out the Dandelion weapon Menlo had taken. "Let's see what this thing can do," she said aiming it at a Dandelion walking in front of her. A blue ball flew across the grass and struck the tall, yellow figure. Nothing happened. She fired again. Same thing. Lenore chose another target and fired at it. That Dandelion kept walking forward too. The blue balls had no effect against their armor.

Nick drew back his bow and shot the same figure in the back. It fell. "I like my weapon better," he smiled at Lenore.

The line of Dandelions finally got within 100 yards of the villagers. "Red bracers, on my mark," Patrick and Jen yelled. They waited until just the right time. "Fire." Two dozen archers shot at once and the arrows whizzed into the targets. There was a loud crunching sound as the bodkin points punched through the yellow armor. All along the yellow line figures crumpled and fell on the grass. The archers notched another volley of arrows on their bows. "Fire," Jen and Patrick yelled. Another group of Dandelions fell. The long yellow line had started out with Dandelions walking should to shoulder. Now, that line had big gaps in it.

"Green bracers, ready," Jen and Patrick called. "Reds, keep firing. Greens, hold steady. Fire." A deadly, whizzing hail, twice as strong as the first, swept into the yellow line. Lots more Dandelions went down. Meanwhile, Mike's and Charlie's groups kept picking off Dandelions from behind.

"Blues, ready," Jen and Patrick yelled. "Reds, greens, fire at will." The thin yellow line was now only 50 yards away. That was perilously close, as their weapons became effective at 40 yards. "Fire blues," they called. Many of the remaining Dandelions fell until only two dozen continued the march forward. They were now in range to use their weapons and they opened fire. Blue balls flew across the field. Some villagers fell. The blue balls were met by another angry hail of arrows.

Finally, only two Dandelions were left standing. They fired their weapons one last time. Two blue balls flew across the short space. One missed; one hit a teenage girl wearing a white bracer. She fell where she stood. Every archer on the field shot at the last two Dandelions at once. Dozens of bodkin points tore apart their yellow armor. They fell backward and lay on the grass looking like yellow pin cushions.

The villagers and the two time crews yelled in joy, jumping up and down and hugging each other. After a long time of celebrating their victory, they looked across the field. At the other end, a small group of Dandelions was standing and watching. The boys knew these were leaders, remaining behind to observe the action. Nick, Patrick, and Mike shouted insults at the distant figures. They gave the group the two fingered salute they had learned from the archers at Agincourt. The group of Dandelions turned and walked back toward Durham.

In the village the victory celebration continued. People danced and sang and congratulated each other. The village had only lost six archers to the blue balls. The family and friends of the six dead stayed in their cottages and cried. The blue balls turned their victims into goo, so there wasn't anything left for their families to bury. There would be no graves those people could visit. In coming days, they set up white crosses and placed flowers where their loved ones had fallen. Patrick and Jen went to each cottage and comforted the families.

The next morning the two time crews and Charlie returned to the field. They were stunned to find all the Dandelion bodies had been removed. Yesterday afternoon 300 yellow figures littered the space. Now, except for some arrows still sticking in the ground and the trampled grass, it was like nothing had happened. The scene was silent and eerie, making the small group of people nervous and even afraid. "What happened?" Patrick asked, surprise and a hint of fear in his voice.

"The Dandelions came out from Durham last night and collected the bodies," Jen said. She was too shocked to realize she was stating the obvious. "Who else would do it?"

"And they did it right under our noses," Mike added with concern. He realized how close the Dandelions had been to the village while they all slept.

Why?" Lenore asked, glancing around nervously, as if afraid the Dandelions were lurking nearby

"Maybe they have feelings and care for each other," Allie wondered, but she said it almost as if asking a question.

"Or, they didn't want us to learn any more about them," Nick added. "Maybe they're afraid we'll find out something."

"Or...." Mike began. "They want to figure out how our weapons work and how they penetrate their armor. They want to learn more about us, and that's not a good thing." Turning to Charlie he said, "We can't allow ourselves to be surprised again like yesterday. Will you meet us at the tables by the butts in one hour? Bring four archers the villagers respect, people they will follow in a fight."

Around the table Patrick said to Charlie, his four friends, and the two time crews, "We were lucky. If Menlo hadn't smelled the Dandelions, things would be very different right now. A lot of people in this village would be dead and the rest of us would be hiding far away from here. The Dandelions would own New Durham.

"We need to set up a round-the-clock guard to watch for another attack. Charlie, when this is all over and we go back to our time, you will be left to lead the archers. I want you to work with me and Jen and learn to be a leader. You four, I want you to become group leaders. We've already divided the archers by color. I want each of you to take charge of a group. You that get the blues and whites, train them until they earn red and green bracers.

"Each group will guard the village for six hours. With four groups, we will be protected all day. Your groups are too big for you to lead all by yourselves. Divide them in half and appoint assistant group leaders you trust. They will help you. Finally, we need to set up an alarm, a bell we can ring when there's an emergency. Charlie, will you take care of that?"

"We don't have a lot to worry about anymore," one of the group leaders said. "Our longbows made short work of those Dandelions."

"We surprised them," Mike said, correcting the group leader. "The Dandelions may be reptiles, but they're intelligent. They developed a lot of technology. We have to assume they're smart enough to learn from their mistakes. We were sent to Agincourt to study how the longbow changed the way armies fought. When the English started using the longbow they could shoot an arrow through French armor. The French responded by making heavier armor. The English countered the heavy armor by using steel bodkins to get through it. That improvement led to the gun. It could shoot through everything.

"The Dandelions will do the same thing. Maybe they will make different armor. Maybe they will attack in a new way so we can't use our arrows. We need to be ready for anything. We have to practice fighting different ways."

"Ideas," Patrick said.

"Today we fought like the English army, standing in rows on a big field," Mike replied. "We need to train to fight in the village, in case they ever get in here. If they force us out of the village, we should be able to fight in the woods. If we want to win this war, someday we're gonna have to go into Durham and force them out. We need to know how to fight like Robin Hood in Sherwood

Forest. We need to know how to ambush them. We need to be able to fight in small groups from behind walls and buildings that will protect us from their weapons."

The time crews trained three groups of archers every day. The fourth group was always on guard. The archers went into the woods to learn to fight there. They built a simulated village they could practice in. They worked out hand signals. This way, they could communicate without being heard or seen. They had a code word for this way of fighting. They called it "Robin Hood."

Old people and children came to watch the practice. The activity was not only interesting; it comforted the villagers to know their fighters were prepared for different types of attack.

A couple of weeks later, a group of greens was on guard duty at the field. One of them pointed toward the city of Durham. The assistant group leader turned and saw ten Dandelions starting across the field. Again, a small group of Dandelion leaders stayed behind and watched. "Sound the alarm," a green archer said.

"Let's wait," the assistant group leader answered. "Those Dandelions are crazy. There are only ten of them. It'll be like shooting fish in a barrel. Let's save the fun for ourselves. We'll be heroes."

The assistant group leader told the archers to form a line. There were only a dozen archers, so it was a short line. However, the line of Dandelions was also short. "Steady," the assistant group leader told his archers as he watched the Dandelions get closer. Green bracers could hit a target at 75 yards. He was waiting for them to get within range.

The greens were so excited at the prospect of another victory they didn't notice that these Dandelions looked different. Their chests were not wide and flat like before. Their armor had two angled sides, making their chests look like the bow on a boat. Their helmets had the same boat shape. When the Dandelions were 75 yards away, the assistant group leader yelled, "Fire." A dozen arrows flew. Each hit a Dandelion in the chest and slid off to the side. The arrows stuck in the ground behind the Dandelions and not in their chests.

"Fire again," the assistant group leader yelled. Same thing. The arrows merely glanced off the angled sides of the Dandelion armor. By now, the Dandelions had gotten too close, forcing the archers to turn and run toward the village. One had the presence of mind to stop and ring the alarm bell, but a blue ball dropped him before he could pull the rope.

The village didn't know of the danger until the green bracers ran through yelling "Attack. Run. Attack." A young child and an old woman came out of the cottage closest to the field. They heard the yelling and wanted to see what was happening. Both fell as blue balls hit them.

Archers grabbed their bows while Jen and Patrick ran to the center of the village to direct the fight. "Robin Hood!" they yelled, telling the archers how to fight. "Robin Hood!" The archers spread out and hid behind the cottages and sheds to ambush the approaching Dandelions. Jen and Patrick waved on the villagers and urged them to run as fast as they could towards the woods. Some archers helped the old people and children escape.

Nick saw an archer shoot at a Dandelion and watched the arrow glance off. Right away, he understood what the Dandelions had done. They had developed a new shape of armor that protected against the bodkin points. "The helmet is connected at the neck," he yelled to Patrick and Jen hiding behind another cottage. "It's a weak point. Aim at it."

Patrick waited until two Dandelions walked past his hiding place. He came out from behind the cottage and shot one in the neck. That worked. It fell. The other Dandelion saw Patrick run back behind the cottage and started to go after him. As it did, Jen came out from the other side of the home and shot it in the neck.

The other archers saw what had happened and did the same thing. In a minute, all ten Dandelions were laying on the ground. "Drag them out of here," Patrick told the archers. "Leave them in the woods. I don't want the children seeing them."

Patrick called Charlie, the group leaders, and the assistant group leaders together. "How did this happen?" he demanded. The green assistant group leader confessed. He said he thought his archers could handle a dozen Dandelions. They thought it would be fun and everyone would be impressed with them.

"You mean you didn't ring the bell because you wanted the glory of beating the Dandelions for yourself?" Patrick snapped. He was angry. The man nodded and hung his head. Anyone who happened on the situation would have thought it strange to see a 14-year old boy chew out an adult. However, Patrick was not just any boy. He had trained at the Time Institute and commanded a time crew. He was used to being in charge. "Jen, Charlie, and I have to go to the family that lives in that first cottage," he hissed at the assistant group leader. "We have to tell them their child and grandmother are dead because you wanted glory.

"Green group leader. Find yourself a new assistant. Find someone who will ring that bell if they see one Dandelion take a step onto that field. Find someone who only thinks about saving this village, not about glory. We're in a war. There's no glory in war. It's a rotten, lousy business. I hate it."

"The Dandelions didn't waste any time," Mike said after Charlie and the archers had left. "Right after the battle in the field they started looking for ways to beat us. They came close this time. When we fought on the field, one archer could drop a bunch of Dandelions. Now, we have to work in teams to kill just one. We would have lost this fight if they had sent fifty with this new armor. They changed the odds in their favor."

"Why didn't they send a lot more?" Lenore asked.

"They wanted to see if the armor worked without losing a bunch of Dandelions," Mike answered. "The leaders saw the arrows bounce off so they know the armor does the job. If the ten had returned safely there would be an army of Dandelions on its way right now. They didn't go back, and the leaders don't know what happened to them once they got into the village. They'll worry we have another weapon and they'll want to think about that for a while.

"The scary thing is we have run out of time. We need to find out what's going on. We need to know why they're here, and what they're doing."

"You gonna try a Vulcan Mind Meld, Mr. Spock?" Patrick asked his S/O. "If you do, I hope it works on dead Dandelions. That's all we've got."

"No," Mike answered. "We need to go into Durham."

CHAPTER TWELVE
A HOT TIME IN THE OLD TOWN

The next morning the two time crews met at the time craft. Jen had painted the word VICTORY on the front. "A pilot gets to choose a craft's name," she said. "I named this one after our victory at the field. It also means I plan to beat the Dandelions in a total victory."

Jen flew the cloaked Victory over the city of Durham, circling slowly so the others could watch out the porthole windows for anything important. "The place sure is run down," Allie said. "It's hard to imagine we went to school here."

"It looks like something is happening over there," Lenore said. Everyone looked where she was pointing, at a long, low building where lots of Dandelions were coming and going.

"That's the hockey arena," Nick said. He recognized the Whittemore Center where the UNH hockey team used to play. "The Dandelions are reptilian and need heat. What would they be doing in a building that was built to stay cold?"

"Make a note," Mike said. "We'll check it out later. Let's see what else is going on." As Jen continued to circle, she slowly moved the Victory out toward the Time Institute. In the distance the two crews could see a tall column of smoke rising high into the air. It went so high it disappeared from view.

"That smoke's coming from the MacDonald Center," Allie observed. "What's going on?" Jen circled slowly over the building while the crews watched. They saw plenty of Dandelions on the ground below them. The yellow figures were working, moving piles of boxes and long tubes into the Center. "I think we should check that place out too," Allie said. "With all that smoke and all that activity, there's no doubt they're up to something."

At that point a large aircraft came down out of the clouds and landed on the old time craft arrival/departure pad, right next to another craft of the same kind. While the Victory circled slowly over the pad, the newly arrived craft opened its doors and the time crews watched dozens of yellow Dandelions march out. Each one was carrying a large box or a tube like the ones being brought into the MacDonald Center. While this was happening, the other craft took off and headed up into the sky. "Pretty safe to say the arrival/departure pad plays an important role in their plan," Mike said.

"I think we've found enough activities that need to be checked out," Patrick added. "Ideas. We need to plan what we're going to do."

"We need to investigate three different places," Mike said. "We should split up. I suggest Allie and I check out the Whittemore Center. Jen, you could drop us off. We'll set a time to pick us up."

"Nick and I can check out the MacDonald Center," Patrick suggested. "Jen, you're the pilot and Lenore's your engineer. You guys should stay with the Victory. Use it to find out where those aircraft are coming from."

Jen set the Victory down in a wooded area near the arena. "Meet us here in one hour," she said to Mike and Allie. She dropped off Nick and Patrick near the MacDonald Center. "One hour, right here," she told them. Then, Lenore and Jen flew over to the arrival/departure pad. They circled twice, keeping an eye on the craft they had seen land. On their third loop the craft rose into the air and took off. Jen followed. The craft continued to rise until Jen and Lenore realized they were going into space. That presented no difficulty for a time craft. The Victory could travel at hyper-light speed and had no trouble keeping up with the vessel.

They followed the Dandelion spaceship for a long time until Jen realized where it was headed. "I've made this trip a lot of times," she said to Lenore. "I think it's going to the wormhole." Sure enough, the Dandelion craft arrived at the entry to the wormhole, where it stopped and waited. Still cloaked, Jen and Lenore did the same, all the while keeping an eye on the Dandelion vessel. Another craft of the same type came out of the worm hole and zipped on by. "I'm betting they're heading for earth," Jen said. "It appears they have a regular shuttle operation going on."

As soon as the opening was clear, the craft they had followed entered the hole. Jen went in after it. The wormhole whizzed by as they moved through it, still following the craft. They came out the other end where Jen decided to end the chase. They had found out what they needed to know. Jen showed Lenore the power plant at the black hole. It was dark and empty. Since humans had stopped time traveling, they didn't need the power plant anymore.

Jen flew the Victory back to earth. "We don't know exactly where the Dandelions come from, but now we know they're extraterrestrials," Lenore said. "We still need to answer some other questions. Why did they come to earth? We know they're not explorers, so what are they up to? It looks like they're in the middle of a big project. What exactly are they doing in Durham?"

As soon as Mike and Allie got out of the Victory a horrible smell passed over them like a cloud. "It's like rotten eggs," Mike said coughing.

"It's sulfur," Allie told him. "I remember that smell from chemistry class back in Ukraine, before I became a cadet at the Time Institute. Once you smell it, you never forget it."

Mike and Allie had no trouble getting into the Whittemore Center. Wearing their cloaked uniforms they simply followed a couple of Dandelions up the stairs and passed through the doors behind them. The cloaked pair of time travelers was surprised the building had no security. "Perhaps this is just a gym or a dormitory," Allie said. "I'm still asking myself Nick's question. What are creatures that need heat doing in a place that's built to stay cold?" The pair walked through another pair of doors and right into the answer. The heat hit them in the face like a slap. Sweat began dripping and their bodies were soon soaked.

Inside, the air smelled even worse than outside. Mike and Allie felt their throats tighten and they had trouble breathing. "Pressurize your suit, Allie," Mike said. "Like in outer space. They must have a different atmosphere in here. It's poisonous to us.

"I won't be able to take this heat very long," he added. "I'll pass out. I hope we find what we came for fast." They did. It happened as they walked through doors that led to the bleachers. There, they looked down at the rink where once there had been a floor of ice. Now, there were rows and rows of round, white objects that looked like soccer balls. The balls were neatly packed, and so close together they touched. There must have been a thousand of them.

The balls were on some sort of serpentine platform or track. They moved slowly so that over time, every row ended up passing along the side of the rink. Lots of Dandelions stood around the edge working. They didn't have on their armor and for the first time Mike and Allie saw what these creatures were like. The Dandelions were gray, but had white chests and bellies. As they worked, some of them turned around revealing to the cloaked time travelers they had yellow stripes on their backs. The pair observed the reptiles had only three fingers and a thumb. The fingers had large claws. Their long forked tongues kept flicking in and out of their mouths.

The Dandelions standing around the arena floor used some kind of tube to examine each ball as it passed on the moving conveyer. Next, they listened to the ball by putting the tube in the ear hole in the side of their heads. Finally, they gently picked up the ball and rolled it in their clawed hands. They examined the entire surface and then carefully replaced it. Mike and Allie watched for a minute. "They chose the Whittemore Center because it's a big, open space," Mike said.

"It's insulated to keep in the cold, so it also keeps in the heat," Allie added. "Come on. We need to check out those balls." They approached the row of moving spheres as the conveyer passed by their side of the arena. They touched some. The balls were smooth.

Mike knocked on one with his knuckles. It wasn't hard. It was rubbery. "It feels like it's full of water," he said.

"It's not water, Mike," Allie said seriously. "I just figured out what they are. They're eggs. This is a giant hatchery. Those are eggs, and each one has a baby in it. They're not just flying in Dandelions. They're breeding. When these eggs hatch, their population is going to get real big, real fast!"

"I gotta get out of here before I die," Mike said. "First, can you spot where all this heat's coming from?"

"That machine over there looks like some sort of pump," Allie said. "It has big hoses running down to the floor. I bet they pump the heat under the eggs."

"It looks like a pretty simple machine," Mike said. "I would have expected something a lot bigger. Let's go. I think I've sweated out ten pounds. I'm feeling light headed. I need fresh air."

Patrick and Nick both gasped as they got out of the Victory. "That smell is awful," Nick said. "It's like rotten eggs. What in the world are they doing in there?" The two time travelers had no trouble getting into the MacDonald Center as the doors were wide open. The Dandelions had left them open to make it easier to carry in all those boxes and tubes. The boys paused in the entry to ponder the bronze plaque dedicating the center to Dr. James A. MacDonald. As cadets, they used to touch it for luck whenever they entered or left the building. No one had cleaned it in a generations and the plaque had corroded and turned green.

Getting into the building was the easy part. Getting around inside would be hard. The first floor was full of boxes, tubes, and Dandelions. Nick examined the boxes. From the air he had not noticed, but there were two different colors, red and blue. The tubes were different too. Some were yellow striped, while others had green stripes.

A line of Dandelions was climbing one side of the stairs, each carrying either a box or tube. Another line was descending the other side of the stairs, empty handed. When they got back down to the first floor the yellow figures picked up another box or tube and got in line to take it upstairs. There was no room for Patrick and Nick to slip by.

"Why walk when you can ride," Nick said as he climbed on top of a box. He waited only a minute before a Dandelion picked it up and carried the box and the invisible Nick upstairs. Patrick watched Nick disappear and climbed on a box too.

Nick and Patrick used to take classes on the second and third floors. They were surprised to see that the classrooms were gone. In fact, the floors were gone. Everything was gone. Above the second floor, the Macdonald Center was a huge empty space. Everything had been taken out to make room for three things: the boxes, the tubes, and an enormous machine.

The line of Dandelions continued moving boxes and tubes up the stairs and stacking them in this huge cave. They made two stacks, one of blue and one of red boxes. They lined up the tubes by the color of their stripes. Other dandelions picked up the tubes and brought them to the machine. They attached the green striped tubes to one side of the machine and the yellow striped ones to the other side. Others carried boxes to the machine. There, they opened the containers and poured the powder from the blue boxes into a big funnel. The boys could see the powder was yellow. They poured the contents of the red boxes into another funnel. That powder was white.

Nick watched all the activity with a frown. "What's going on," Patrick asked him with concern. He realized none of this held any hope of a happy outcome for the people of New Durham.

"I'm not sure," Nick answered. "I know this machine is responsible for the big cloud we saw. I need to get closer to it to figure out its purpose." The boys moved to the place where the tubes were attached. Inside the machine they could see a white flame, so bright it hurt to look at it. They had to close their eyes and let them readjust to the dim light inside the building. "Acetylene," Nick said when he could open his eyes again. Don't look at the flame. It can damage your eyes. These tubes are gas cylinders. The green stripes are acetylene. The yellow stripes have to be oxygen. If you burn them together you get a really hot flame. My grandpa and I use an acetylene torch for cutting steel when we're restoring cars. We have to wear really dark glasses to protect our eyes."

"Why are they burning this stuff?" Patrick asked, shading his eyes with his hand.

"I'm only an engineer," Nick replied. "I'll find out what they're doing, but I'll leave it to Mike and Allie to figure out why. Now that we know what's in the tubes, we need to examine those boxes." The boys walked back to the where the containers were stacked. One Dandelion was opening boxes for the others to carry to the funnels. Nick reached into a blue box and took off his glove. He picked up some of the yellow powder and poured it into his glove. Then, he put the glove back on. He went to a red box and put some white powder into his other glove. "I think we've seen enough," Nick said to Patrick. "We should get outside to meet the Victory."

Patrick stared at the stairs. "We're not gonna get down that way. It's covered with Dandelions." He walked to a window and looked out. "It's only about twelve feet to the ground," he said. "If we hang onto the window sill and lower ourselves down, we'll only have to drop about six feet. We'll land in the grass. It should be soft enough so we don't get hurt."

On the ground the boys went to the pickup point. The Victory's door opened and they climbed in. Jen and Lenore had already picked up Mike and Allie. The pilot flew the craft back to New Durham.

CHAPTER THIRTEEN

BOOM!

Back in the village the two time crews went to the butts and sat down at one of the picnic tables. They waited for Charlie and the group leaders to join them. When they were all together Patrick described to Charlie and his friends how the time crews had split up in Durham and spied on Dandelion activities. "Now, we're gonna compare notes," he said. "You should know what we saw, and then hear what we think it means. It's your future that's at risk."

"We know where the Dandelions come from," Jen told the group. "Well, maybe not exactly where, but we know they're not from another dimension, and they're not time travelers. They're extraterrestrials. They're from another planet. They're getting here through the wormhole. They have a fleet of spaceships going through there, one after another. It's a round-the-clock shuttle service."

Patrick explained the wormhole to Charlie and the group leaders. He told them how important the passage way once was to time travel. Time craft used it to get to the power plant at the black hole. There, they recharged so they could travel at hyper-light speed.

"We know the spaceships arrive loaded with Dandelions and supplies," Jen continued. "We don't know how long they've been doing this, but it's been going on for a while. They've brought in some serious equipment and they didn't manage all that in a couple of flights."

Allie spoke next. She explained what she and Mike had observed at the hockey rink. "They're not just flying in Dandelions," she said. "They're raising the next generation in there. We don't know how long it will be before those eggs start hatching. When they do, we're going to have more Dandelions than we can handle. We'll have to hope their young take a long time to grow up."

"If the Dandelions are gonna hatch their children and raise them here, we have to figure they plan on staying," Mike added. "They didn't come to earth to take something and then leave."

Nick told the group what was going on in the MacDonald Center. "They have a huge factory in there," he said. "Dozens of Dandelions are at work carrying in those boxes and tubes. We learned the tubes are gas cylinders and that they hold acetylene and oxygen. We don't know what the powders are, but I got some samples." He pulled off his gloves and poured the powders onto a piece of paper.

"I know the yellow powder," Allie said. "It's sulfur. That's why the air in Durham smells so bad. They're burning sulfur." She took a pinch of the white powder and sniffed it. She rubbed it between her fingertips. "I don't know what this is," she said. "I might be able to figure it out if I had a chemistry lab."

"Why are they doing this?" Nick asked. "It's a huge factory. They put a lot of time and work into building it. It has to be important to them, and what's important to them is usually bad news for us."

"Oh, it's bad news for sure," Mike said with a grimace. "Really bad news. Allie and I tried to breathe the air in the arena. It's poisonous to us, but it's not to them. The Dandelions working in there didn't wear armor. They've created their home world's atmosphere in there, the kind of air they need to breath. I'm sure it's the air their eggs need to hatch. That's their environment."

"They wear their armor to protect themselves from our air," Allie realized. "That means their armor is a type of space suit and they can't live on earth without it. It keeps them warm and it gives them the mixture of chemicals they need to breathe."

"Exactly," Mike said with excitement as he fit the parts of the puzzle together in his mind. "That's why they're burning those chemicals. They're pumping our air full of the chemicals they need. They're changing our atmosphere so they can breathe it."

"Won't that kill us?" Charlie asked.

"Yes," Allie said. "It will kill all the humans on earth and most of the animals. Then, earth will belong to the Dandelions. You're right Mike. They are here to stay. In fact, they're making themselves right at home."

"Yeah," Mike said in agreement. "One more thing. The earth is too cool for them. They need it hot. I'm sure that cloud is making lots of greenhouse gases. They plan on raising the temperature too. When they're done, earth will be a Dandelion paradise."

"That's why they never tried to wipe you out," Patrick said to Charlie. "They killed any people they found, but that's all. They only killed you when they needed to get you out of the way. They know that changing the air and heating up the planet will take care of the rest of those pesky humans. They plan to make us extinct."

"Longbows and arrows aren't going to help us in the end," Charlie said grimly. Everyone at the meeting stared at the table in resignation. A handful of villagers were no match for the massive Dandelion project.

"We need to call in the Army," Nick said sarcastically. "They have lots of big guns that could blow Durham into dust."

"The Air Force could bomb it off the map," Patrick said with a frown.

"The Navy would use cruise missiles," Mike added with the same lack of hope. Everyone looked at the boys and wondered what they were talking about. "That's how we would have handled the Dandelions in our time," Mike explained. "We had weapons that would blow them all up. Too bad you guys don't have any bombs, Charlie. They really work well at times like this."

"I'm afraid we've finally run out of audacity and innovativeness," Patrick said wearily to the two time crews. "We've had a good run, but this is the end of the road."

That night Mike lay in bed and listened to Nick snore. He wrestled with the unavoidable disasters that were coming and asked himself what he and his friends should do. He was so unsure. He wished Rabbi Cohen was here to give him the answers. If the two crews got into the Victory and went back to their own time, then they would be safe. Humanity would be wiped out, but they would be safely in the past where they belonged. After all, this was not their time and this was not really their fight. They had their own lives to live.

"We would live if we returned," Mike said to himself. "But our actions would prove us to be cowards, and I don't want to live like that. We can't run out on our friends. I don't want that on my conscience. We've never done anything like that. We've always been loyal."

Mike continued to struggle with his thoughts. If they stayed and were loyal to their friends they would die with the rest of the humans on earth. They would witness the end of time with all these people they cared about, even though it would be the last thing they witnessed. Mike thought about all the things he would never do if Patrick's and Jen's crews stayed. The Sirens would never play again. He would never develop Chamber Rock. He would never get married and have his own children. He would never go to high school. He laughed to himself. He would never turn in the paper he had to write about life during the Civil War.

Sometime later Mike woke with a start from a deep sleep. "Patrick. Nick," he called to his friends. "Wake up, guys." They stirred and sat up. Patrick lit a candle. "I know how to make a bomb," Mike said. "Get a good night's sleep. We're back in business, and tomorrow morning New Durham will witness the grand opening of the Time Institute Bomb Factory."

After breakfast the time crews, Charlie, and the group leaders met at the butts. "Charlie," Mike said. "We know how to build the bombs we need to fight the Dandelions. I've been studying life in the southern states during the American Civil War. When the southerners ran out of supplies they had to make their own gunpowder so they could keep fighting. They used the gunpowder in their rifles, but they made bombs with it too.

"Gunpowder is real simple. We only need three things. We need charcoal. I saw the collier making charcoal in Hilton and he showed me how it was done. We need sulfur. We know the Dandelions have huge amounts of it. We will steal some from them. And we need saltpeter. This part is a little gross. I need you to tell the people in New Durham to save their pee. It just became real valuable."

"Charlie," Patrick said. "The archers will be the best people to take on these responsibilities. They're already used to working together. You should be in charge, and be the guy who makes sure all the jobs get done. Group leaders, each of your groups will take on one job. One group will cut down trees for charcoal. One group will work with Mike to make a charcoal kiln. Another group will take the pee and dry it. The last group will have to collect the saltpeter.

"Time crews," Patrick said to his friends. "We need to go back into Durham and get some sulfur. Jen, will you fly Nick and me back to the MacDonald Center? We should go tonight. It will be easier to help ourselves to their sulfur when it's dark."

"I don't think even three of us can carry one of those boxes," Nick said. "It would be too heavy. I suggest we take some cloth bags and some rope. We can fill the bags and lower them out the window."

That night, Jen set the Victory down beside the MacDonald Center. Nick and Patrick got out of the craft and went around to the front of the building. Work had ended for the day. The Dandelions were gone, but the doors were still open. Out front was a pile of empty boxes and tubes. "I'll bet those are going back on the next flight to be filled again," Nick told Patrick. He picked up one of the boxes and carried it back to the Victory. "We'll fill it one bag at a time," he told Jen.

Upstairs a small group of Dandelions was still working, changing the cylinders and pouring the boxes of sulfur and the other chemical into the big funnels. Nick and Patrick hid behind a box of sulfur and began to shovel the powder into a bag. They tied a rope to the bag and lowered it out the window to Jen, who took the bag and carried it to the Victory. She emptied the sulfur into the box and came back with the empty bag just as another full one was lowered to the ground. She took the full bag and tied the empty one to the rope. Up it went to be refilled.

When the box was full Nick and Patrick walked back down the stairs and out the front door. Nick paused for a moment and examined the pile of tubes. Let's take a couple," he suggested to Patrick. "They're shaped like bombs. Maybe that's what they'll become."

In a week, the charcoal was ready and Mike emptied the kiln. He showed the archers how to use flat rocks to grind the charcoal into powder. Then, he mixed the charcoal powder with sulfur and saltpeter. He poured a small pile of the mixture on the ground and touched a flame to it. *Woooosh.* The powder burned instantly, making a big cloud of smoke that the wind carried across the village. Mike smiled and everyone clapped him on the back.

"I'm going to make lots and lots of this stuff," Mike said. "Nick, Lenore, you're the engineers. I'll give the gunpowder to you guys. It'll be your job to figure out how to make bombs and to blow up stuff. Have fun."

The people of New Durham got used to booms, bangs, and pops coming from the butts. They got used to the smelly clouds of gun smoke drifting across the village. They got used to seeing Nick and Lenore with soot-covered faces.

A week went by and Nick asked Patrick to gather the crews, Charlie, and the group leaders at the butts. "We want to show you what we've been working on," Nick told the group as he placed a pile of small packages on the table. "These bombs will blow a hole in a wall. If you want to knock down a building, you can use them to blow apart the beams that hold it up. I brought duct tape with me." He showed the group a large, gray roll of the stuff. Patrick, Mike, Jen, and Allie were the only ones who knew what it was. They had used duct tape to tie up Dr. Morley and his minions on their first mission. "The tape will hold a bomb in place," Nick continued. "That means we can secure explosives anywhere we want to place them.

"We've worked out some timed fuses so we can set the bombs to blow up when we want. This means we can get far away from the explosion before it detonates. Mike, Patrick you know what caps are, the rolls of red paper with the little dots on them. You hit a dot and it goes bang. We've made some caps and put them into other bombs so they work as hand grenades, only better. If you throw our grenade, the cap fires when the bomb hits something. It explodes on contact. No waiting.

"We put some of those cap fuses in the tubes we took from the MacDonald Center. That means we can drop these tubes from the Victory and bomb targets, just like the air force.

"Finally, Lenore's gonna show you my favorite bomb." Nick had everyone stand up. Then, he tipped the heavy picnic table so it stood on one end. He led the group a distance away from the table. "Watch," he said. "You're gonna like this." Lenore had a longbow. She put an arrow on the bow and aimed at the table top. The group noticed that the arrow didn't have a bodkin point. Instead, the end was a small tube about the size of a colored marker. Lenore shot the arrow at the table top. When it hit there was a boom and a cloud of smoke. When the smoke cleared everyone saw a big hole in the thick table top.

"I don't care how strong the Dandelions make their armor," Nick said proudly. "I don't care what shape they make it. These arrows will blow it open. If the explosion doesn't take care of the

Dandelion inside, it will still lose its atmosphere. It'll die quickly because it can't breathe our air."

"Nick and Lenore, you just evened the odds," Patrick said proudly. "Let's take this war to the Dandelions. They messed with the wrong planet."

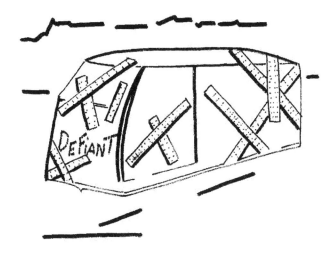

CHAPTER FOURTEEN
SUICIDE

"There are two priority targets we have to take out," Patrick said to the time crews. "First, we need to shut down the MacDonald Center smoke factory. That will stop the Dandelions from changing the air and heating up the planet. Second, we have to take care of the hatchery at Whittemore Center. We don't want thousands more Dandelions joining the fight."

"What stops them from building another factory and another hatchery?" Allie asked. "Even if we take care of those two targets, we've only delayed the Dandelions. They'll start all over again. They'll become a lot more careful and it'll be harder to knock them out again the next time."

"She's right," Mike added. "We have a leak in our boat and we need to fix that leak before we start bailing out the water."

"How do we stop their space craft?" Patrick asked. "The Victory's not built for fighting. We're not gonna blow them out of the sky with arrow bombs."

Everyone sat silent for a long time. The others knew Mike and Allie were right. It wouldn't do any good to knock out the smoke plant and the hatchery first. The Dandelions would soon build new ones. Then, they would be on their guard and protect their facilities more carefully than they were doing now. The crews would never get a second chance to attack.

Allie spoke. "I know this is tough for us to think about, but is there any way to destroy the wormhole?" All the time travelers knew the wormhole. They had passed through it many times. They had first learned about the wormhole when they were cadets taking Rabbi Cohen's *History of Time Travel* class. It's a tunnel in space discovered early in the history of time travel. It was instrumental in making time travel possible. One end is near earth. The other end is hundreds of light years away in distant space, near a black hole. Time craft use the black hole's reverse gravity to push the craft at hyper-light speed. The craft are recharged at a factory built near the black hole. Without the wormhole, they couldn't get to the factory.

"You can't do that," everyone said at once.

"How would we time travel?" Patrick asked.

Mike understood Allie's thinking. "We would still time travel, in our time," he said. "We would only be making it impossible for humans to ever time travel from this time on. Remember guys, they don't time travel now. If the Dandelions have their way, in a little while there won't be any humans left to time travel. Allie's idea is real hard to swallow, because the wormhole is so important to us. The Dandelions aren't giving us many choices. This is life or death. We're talking about extinction. We're talking about human beings disappearing forever. All options have to be on the table. We have to talk about this."

"I know humans don't time travel now," Lenore said. "But what if they want to do it again in the future? We would have changed things so it could never happen again."

"We're at a crossroads," Allie argued. "We have to choose one thing or the other. We can't have both. Maybe humans will want to time travel again someday. Maybe they won't. If they're all dead, it doesn't matter what they would choose to do, because they're not going to be around to do it."

"I'm not comfortable making that decision for them," Jen answered. "Won't we be changing the future?"

"We would be giving humanity back its future," Mike argued. "Remember, with the way things are going these people are pretty close to the end of time. If humanity survives, it is up to them to do what they want with the future. The only thing we will have taken away is the ability to time travel. I think the choice is pretty clear.

Live and not do something you're not doing anyway, or die. I know what I'd choose."

Once again, the group was silent as they pondered the choice they faced. Grim reality set in as they realized they had to think the unthinkable.

"Even if we wanted to close the wormhole how would we do it?" Jen asked.

Nick raised his hand. "We're not in class, Nick," Patrick said. "You don't have to raise your hand. What's your idea?"

"A huge explosion inside the wormhole," Nick said. "We could try to blow it up."

"Okay," Patrick answered. "Let's say an explosion would close the wormhole. How do we make that happen? Remember, it's in outer space."

"We could fill a time craft with bombs and fly it in," Nick said. "Inside the wormhole, we set off the bombs. I don't know if it would work, but we could try."

"Nick," Jen said to the engineer. "All we have is the Victory. It would be a suicide mission. Whoever flew it in couldn't get out. The rest of us could never go back to our time."

"When Charlie ran to the hanger and broke in the door, he said he saw a long row of time craft. Remember?" Lenore asked.

Patrick nodded his head. "Okay. Let's say we have another craft. What then?"

"We have two pilots, you and Jen," Mike replied. "You fly two craft into the wormhole; one of them is full of bombs. Inside the wormhole you both pressurize your uniforms and open your craft. The pilot with the bombs goes over to the escape craft. You set off the bombs and get out fast."

"Problem," Allie said. "I learned in chemistry lab that an explosion is a very fast fire. Fires need oxygen to burn. If you open your craft's door you'll lose all your air. An explosion can't happen in space."

"We could send more oxygen with the craft," Nick said. "The Dandelions have tons of it in those tubes. We could steal one. They're not well guarded."

"Have we missed anything?" Patrick asked the group. They all shook their heads. They had a good plan. "Okay. Jen and Lenore, will you take Nick and me to the hanger tonight in the Victory? I'll fly another time craft back here and Nick can get it ready for the wormhole."

That night Jen and Lenore flew Patrick and Nick to the time craft hanger. Jen landed in front of the building near the door where recently, so many young villagers had been gunned down helping Charlie to escape. Patrick and Nick stepped out fully cloaked. The door was hanging open. It had been damaged in the fight and could no longer be closed. The Fixer pilot and engineer were not prepared for the scene in the hanger. They had expected to choose a craft and be out in seconds. Instead, parts and pieces of time craft were thrown all over the hanger. The boys knew what had happened; the Dandelions had made sure no one else could escape. They had destroyed the entire fleet.

Patrick and Nick looked at the mess. This was not part of the plan. In fact, right now, there no longer was a plan. Nick picked up a piece of time craft hull and walked back to the Victory with Patrick. "Take us back," Patrick said quietly to Jen, discouragement in his voice. "The Dandelions outsmarted us. The time craft are all cut to pieces."

Mike and Allie were stunned at the news. All that planning had been wasted. The crews sat and talked for a while, but no one could come up with any other ideas for blowing up the wormhole. The only option was a suicide mission. Patrick or Jen would have to fly the Victory into the wormhole and blow up the craft. The two crews would be stranded in the future with no way to get back to their own times.

Jen said she would do the job. "No way," Patrick replied abruptly. "I'll do it.

"Why," Jen demanded, "because you're the guy? You think you have to be the hero?"

When Jen got excited she spoke rapidly and her strong New Zealand accent kicked in. None of her friends could understand her. "Slow down, Jen," Allie said. Jen glared in anger as she took a deep breath.

"I've flown more missions," Patrick argued.

"Then you're the more valuable pilot," Jen answered, speaking deliberately and precisely so the other team leader would know just where she stood. "The Institute needs you more than me. Besides, I'm the Victory's pilot. It's my craft. I call the shots. If it's sacrificed, I will be the one to go with it."

Patrick grimaced. He didn't want to let Jen go, but she kept coming up with better arguments.

"We should flip a coin," Patrick said, making one last try.

"I don't have one, and you don't either," Jen answered.

The group fell silent. They were as sad now as if Jen had already taken the Victory into the wormhole. They knew that soon they would never be together again.

"Please get the Victory ready, Nick," Jen said finally. "I'll go as soon as you're done. It won't be any fun waiting, and I want to get it over with."

Nick glanced at Lenore. "We'll get to it first thing in the morning," he said quietly.

The next morning Nick and Lenore met at the Victory. Nick had brought the piece of a time craft with him. He sat down at a picnic table with Lenore beside him. "I don't want to do this," he said with tears in his eyes.

"I don't either," Lenore replied. She put her face in her hands. "Oh Jen, Jen, Jen," she sobbed.

"In my time we had these things called Smart Bombs," Nick said. "That's what you and I are about to make, a smart bomb. In fact, it will be the smartest bomb ever. Jen is a real smart person and a great pilot, and we have to help her blow herself up. What a waste."

"She's a good friend, too," Lenore answered.

"What if we just said no," Nick suggested. "What if we refuse to get the Victory ready?"

"Then the Dandelions win and everyone else dies," Lenore answered.

"The needs of the many outweigh the needs of the few," Nick said. Lenore looked at him because she didn't understand. "It's something this guy Mr. Spock said," Nick explained. "He was a character on a show named *Star Trek*. It's what he said when he sacrificed his life to save his friends. It sounded a lot better when an actor was speaking a line from a script and it was just pretend." The two stared at the ground a long time without speaking.

Nick repeatedly passed the chunk of time craft from hand to hand. It was a nervous action to occupy his mind and keep it off the horror of the task at hand. It worked. He stopped suddenly and stared at the piece of time craft he was holding. "Let's go get Patrick and Jen," he said to Lenore. "I have an idea."

"Guys," Nick said to the two pilots. "I want you two to fly Lenore and me to the hanger. We need to go in daylight so we can see what we're doing. Bring some longbows. Bring bodkin points and bomb points. We'll be working for a while and we'll need you to protect us."

"What's up," Patrick asked.

"Don't get your hopes up," Nick said, his worried expression even more pronounced than normal. "I wanna try something. It's just a crazy idea, but go along with me. I gotta know if it will work before Jen makes a suicide mission."

Jen set the Victory down on top of the hanger. On the pad, another load of Dandelions had just arrived. They were walking down the ramp from a spaceship, carrying boxes and tubes. Under cloak, Jen and Patrick watched from the roof. They were armed and had arrows ready to drop any Dandelion that came near the hanger, but that didn't look likely. The yellow figures were all busy unloading one craft and carrying empty tubes and boxes onto another.

Nick opened a cupboard in the Victory and pulled out a box of his own. Lenore climbed down from the roof and Nick handed her the box. He climbed down to join her and together they went into the hanger through the damaged door. A couple of hours passed, but Nick and Lenore never came out of the hanger. Once in a while Patrick and Jen heard a noise in the building below, but most of the time things were quiet. All the activity was the Dandelions working on the pad.

At last Nick came out of the hanger and called up to the two pilots on the roof. "Patrick, can you come down?" he asked. Patrick climbed down and followed Nick through the door. He was stunned to see a complete time craft in the hanger, the laser saw cuts all repaired with long strips of duct tape. "My grandpa always says, 'You can fix anything with duct tape,'" Nick said proudly. "We've run some tests and they indicate this thing should work. I need you to fly it back to New Durham. I'll do the finishing touches there. Lenore, will you climb back up on the roof and return in the Victory with Jen?"

Nick gave Patrick the craft's remote and they waited for Lenore to signal that she and Jen were ready to go. Then, Patrick answered the math problem and programmed in the New Durham coordinates. He set the repaired craft down beside the butts. He landed right next to the Victory, just as Allie and Mike arrived from the village. Patrick jumped out. "Will you guys get Charlie and the group leaders?" he asked the two S/Os.

Now that the crews had time to relax they stared at the new craft. It looked strange with strips of duct tape all over it, holding the pieces together. Patrick and Mike laughed and made jokes. "It sure looks like it lost the fight," Mike said.

"Did it get the license number of the truck that ran it over?" Patrick laughed.

"The hard part was finding all the pieces," Nick explained. "All the craft in the hanger had been cut up and tossed around. It was like doing a big jigsaw puzzle. Once we had identified all the pieces for this one craft, it didn't take all that long to tape them together."

"Do you think this thing will hold up?" Patrick asked. He had an interest in the answer, as he was the guy who had to fly it.

"It only has to make one mission," Nick explained.

"It only has to make half a mission," Mike laughed. "It's going, but it's not coming back. When we're done, it'll be in a lot more pieces than when the Dandelions finished with it."

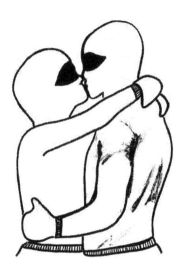

CHAPTER FIFTEEN
JEN AND PATRICK SITTING IN A
TREE

The two crews, Charlie, and the group leaders sat around a picnic table. It was the one with the big hole in the top made by the arrow bomb. Patrick had printed the name DEFIANT on the front of the new craft with duct tape. "A pilot gets to name his craft," he said. "I named it Defiant because it defied the odds by just being here. Also, it'll defy the Dandelions.

"Tell us your plan, Nick," he said to his engineer.

"I made a schedule of all the jobs we need to do," Nick said. "We have two craft. The Defiant is kinda shaky. It has to do its mission, but I don't want to use it for anything else.

"I need a bunch of empty tubes to make the bombs, and I need a full oxygen tube. We'll have to use the Victory to get these things. It has the supercharger, so it can carry a lot more weight. Once we get the bombs, remote, and timer ready I'll have to transfer the supercharger from the Victory to the Defiant so it can carry the load. Then, you and Jen make the mission."

"Problem," Allie said. "When Patrick blows up the Defiant, we lose the supercharger. Then, the Victory can't carry the load it needs to take care of the targets in Durham."

"Right," Nick agreed. "I didn't think of that. Patrick, I'll show you how to disconnect the supercharger. Once you're in the wormhole you'll come to a full stop. At that point you'll no longer need the extra power. Whatever you do, don't forget the equipment and leave it in the Defiant. Jen, make sure he brings that supercharger back with him."

That evening, Jen delivered the boys to the MacDonald Center. The Dandelion workers had piled the empty tubes outside the building, ready to take back to the pad the next day. The boys stowed as many tubes in the Victory as it could hold, careful to leave room for just one more. Then, they went up to the factory.

They threw a cloak cover over an oxygen tube and walked right out the front door with it.

The next day, Lenore and Nick packed the tubes with gunpowder and the archers loaded them into the Defiant. Nick gave Patrick a remote that would set off the bombs. Then, he explained to the pilot the procedure he would need to follow. "On the way to the wormhole, wear your full uniform: head cover and gloves. If the Defiant breaks up in space you want to be fully protected. Remember, before you leave the Defiant, open the oxygen bottle. Give the oxygen a while to fill the cabin. Then, push this button. It is the ignition. Don't stay to watch the fireworks, or you could go up along with them. It would be a good idea if Jen already had the Victory flying toward the end of the wormhole before you set off the bombs."

Patrick took off piloting the supercharged Defiant and Jen followed him in the Victory. When they arrived at the wormhole they found a Dandelion ship waiting at the end near earth. They watched until another ship came out of the wormhole on its way to Durham. Then, the waiting ship entered and disappeared. "Good timing," Jen told Patrick, speaking ship-to-ship through their uniform intercom. "We have the wormhole all to ourselves for a while."

"I'm thinking about going halfway through," Patrick told Jen. "I'm hoping a blast in the middle will suck in both ends."

At about the halfway point, Patrick came to a full stop. Jen pulled up next to him and turned the Victory so it was headed back toward earth. This way, the crafts' two doors were facing each other. "I'm removing the supercharger," Patrick told Jen. "Done," he said a minute later. "I've got it all packed up. I'm opening the oxygen tank. Open the Victory's door."

Patrick looked out a porthole window and saw Jen in the doorway waving to him. He stood back so he would not be sucked out when he opened his own door. Jen picked up a longbow and an arrow. She tied a rope to the arrow and shot it into the Defiant. Patrick picked up his end and tied the rope around his waist. He had the supercharger under his arm. He had the Defiant's remote and the bomb remote in his pocket.

Using the rope, Jen pulled Patrick across to the Victory. In space he had no weight and it was easy. Once inside Jen's craft Patrick used the remote to close the Defiant's door. "It's filling with oxygen," he said. Jen closed the Victory's door and programmed in the coordinates for New Durham.

"I'm ready to go when you decide to blow it up," she told Patrick.

"Let's give it a minute to be sure there's lots of oxygen in there," he said. "I'll count down. On zero, we both push the buttons. We should be able to run ahead of the shock wave. Ready? Five, four, three, two, one, zero." The Victory took off at near light speed. Behind them Jen and Patrick watched a wall of orange fire following them through the wormhole.

The Victory flew safely out the end of the wormhole. Jen made a wide circle and the Victory came to a full stop a safe distance away. The explosion shot out the end of the wormhole like a cannon going off. The long cloud of orange flame blew off into space. The flame disappeared and for a moment the wormhole looked as if nothing had happened. Jen and Patrick were worried. Maybe their plan hadn't worked.

The wormhole began to quiver. Then, it began to shake. Suddenly, the wormhole broke into two pieces. It split right where the explosion had happened. The two pieces began to shrink. They collapsed, shriveled, and disappeared.

Jen and Patrick jumped up and down in excitement. Jen threw her arms around Patrick's neck and kissed him where his lips would be. She couldn't kiss his lips because they were both wearing head covers. They couldn't take off the head covers because Jen had let out all the Victory's air when she had opened the door.

Poor Patrick was completely surprised. He was surprised by Jen and he was surprised by what he did. He put his arms around Jen and pulled her to him. He kissed her right back through his head cover, a long, long kiss.

"I always liked you, Patrick," Jen said to him, looking at his eyes through the lens in his head cover. "Ever since we were cadets."

"Yeah," Patrick said with a smile that Jen could not see. "Me too. I just didn't know what to do. Thanks for breaking the ice." They kissed again. Actually, they just pressed their head covers together. They kissed lots of times in this very odd way.

"I don't want to stop," Jen said. "But we do need to go back and tell the others we did it."

Patrick agreed. "We're pilots," he said. "We do our duty. I guess for us duty will always come first. I really do like you, Jen. The others are all my friends, but you're another pilot. You understand me. You always know what I'm thinking and how I feel."

Jen set the Victory down by the butts. Out the portholes the two pilots could see a crowd of villagers waiting for news, anxious to find out what had happened. Jen opened the door and she and Patrick stepped out holding hands. They both held out their free hands with their thumbs up. The villagers didn't know what they meant, but the two crews did. "You did it. You did it!" Lenore and Allie, said jumping up and down. The villagers understood the girls' excitement and broke out in cheers, everyone hugging each other. The crowd of villagers pushed forward, trying to touch Jen and Patrick.

The archers lifted the two pilots and placed them on their shoulders. They carried Jen and Patrick through New Durham with a parade of villagers following them. It was like Jen and Patrick had just pitched the World Series, or won the Super Bowl.

Other villagers returned to their houses and came out carrying food and drink. They set up a picnic at the butts, and soon all of New Durham was having a party. The only ones not enjoying themselves were the red bracer archers. It was their turn to be on guard. The other archers made up plates of food and glasses of punch for the sentries and brought them to the field.

Patrick and Jen sat under a tree holding hands. Mike and Allie, Nick and Lenore walked over to them. "It looks like the bomb wasn't the only fireworks you set off on that mission," Allie said to her friend. "How did this happen?"

"I think it was always there," Jen answered. "We just needed the right moment." Patrick blushed.

"Well, love birds," Mike said. "We need to talk about where we go from here. It won't be long before the Dandelions are wondering why the next ship didn't arrive. The ship on the pad will head back and won't be able to find the wormhole. They may think something natural closed it. One the other hand, they may figure out we did it. Anyway, they will have to change their plans. I would rather attack them before they can prepare."

"Have you figured out how we're going to blow up the factory?" Patrick asked Nick.

"Yup," Nick said. "I'm going to let them do it for me."

"Huh?" everyone said at once.

"You're gonna love this mission," Nick answered. "We have to go into Durham tonight and do it. I have the bombs all ready. I just need to put the supercharger back into the Victory. We can't go until after dark, so enjoy your free time and have a good afternoon."

At sunset Nick had the Victory prepared for the attack on the factory. The archers had loaded eight bombs. The two time crews climbed aboard and Jen set the Victory down beside the MacDonald Center. "You and Lenore should stay with the craft in case of an emergency," Patrick said to Jen. "The rest of us have done this work before. We should be okay."

Nick, Patrick, Mike, and Allie unloaded six of the eight bombs made from empty acetylene and oxygen tubes. "I want to leave two tubes in the craft," Nick explained. "Just in case." He and his companions placed the six on the ground and threw cloak covers over two of them. Each time traveler picked up an end of a cloaked tube. The four carried two bombs into the building and up the stairs. The MacDonald Center was empty. Just like every other evening, the Dandelion workers had finished for the day and had gone. The only Dandelions in the building were the ones running the smoke machine. The cloaked time travelers placed the tubes at the beginning of the piles and returned to the craft and carried up another pair of tubes. Finally, they brought in the third pair.

"This is the plan," Nick explained to the other three. "There are six acetylene tubes attached to one side of the smoke machine. Six oxygen tubes attached to the other side. They only use three of each at a time. When those three tubes become empty they switch the machine to the three full ones. Then, they replace the empty tubes.

"I figure we'll put three bombs at the front of the acetylene line and another three at the head of the oxygen row. The next time they change the tubes, they will attach our bombs to the machine. We'll watch to make sure they take the right tubes. Then, we get outta here. I programmed the remote to 30 seconds. Half a minute after I push the button, that machine will be a smoking pile of scrap."

The cloaked time travelers rested against a wall and watched the tubes, making sure the Dandelions attached their bombs to the machine. Meanwhile, Mike became bored and began to poke around in the boxes. "Hey," he called. "Look at this." The others peered into the box he was pointing to. It was full of Dandelion weapons.

"Makes sense," Patrick said. "They keep sending in more Dandelions, so they have to bring more weapons."

"Yeah," Mike replied. "But why did they bring them here to the MacDonald Center?" He wandered around seeking more information. He approached a long row of lockers on one wall and quietly opened a door. "Here's the answer," he told the others. They came over to see what the S/O had discovered. The locker was full of weapons. "They're using this as the arsenal, the place they store their guns."

"Look at that," Allie said. Along with the hand weapons were devices that looked like rifles. "I'll bet those have a longer range.

They won't have to get within bowshot to kill us." The next locker had even larger weapons with tripods that would support them when set up.

"Those look like machine guns," Nick commented. "They've brought in some serious firepower. We've given them so much heartburn; I'll bet they plan to use them on us."

"They stay one step ahead of us when it comes to weapons," Mike said with a grimace. "We can't fight against all the power they have here. Even arrow bombs would be useless. Good thing we shut down the wormhole. Have you guys noticed, the Dandelions don't seem to know yet?"

"They'll know tomorrow when the next flight doesn't show up," Nick replied. "They'll realize we've cut them off from their home planet. By that time they'll have also lost this factory and all the weapons in it. They couldn't have stored these things in a worse place. Best place for us, worst place for them."

The four time travelers watched the Dandelion workers replace the empty tubes on their machine. Just as Nick predicted, they selected and attached the bombs, unaware that they had just accomplished a key step in the engineer's plan. With the bombs in place, the time travelers ran down the stairs and out the front door, Nick carrying the remote.

Lenore and Jen had stepped away from the Victory. They were by the MacDonald Center's front door, keeping guard. The boys and Allie ran out of the building and toward the Victory. "Let's go," Nick said as he passed Jen and Lenore. "As soon as we're in the craft I'm going to push the button."

At that moment the two time crews lit up like they were in a spotlight. They still had on their night vision goggles, but the world was no longer black and white. They could see each other like it was broad daylight. "What the….," Patrick said. Everyone realized at once, some kind of beam was shining on them and they were no longer invisible.

They saw where the beam was coming from, a group of Dandelions that was walking towards them. The line of yellow figures had gotten between the crews and the Victory and the crews had nowhere to go but to back up. They backed up and backed up. Eventually, they backed into the MacDonald Center wall, a long way from their craft.

"They do stay one step ahead of us," Mike said. "They must have figured out that invisible people were coming into Durham and they came up with a way to find us. I don't know why they haven't blasted us with blue balls."

"They're under orders to take us prisoner," Allie said. "They realize we know a lot. We're more valuable alive than as puddles of goo." A Dandelion held out his hand to Nick in a gesture that said "Give me the object in your hand." Nick didn't hand it over. Instead, they watched the row of seven Dandelions get closer and closer.

CHAPTER SIXTEEN
RAZZLE DAZZLE

The row of Dandelions formed a solid, moving wall of yellow that trapped the time crews between it and the building. "We gotta get away from here," Nick said. "If I push the button, we'll get blown up with the MacDonald Center."

"Cadets, double reverse," Mike called. "On double go." The two crews understood Mike; he had just called a football play. Having practiced that play over and over, they responded. Nick tossed the remote to Mike and moved behind the quarterback. The rest got into formation. "Go. Go," Mike yelled. Jen ran behind Mike from the left. He turned and pretended to hand off to her. The Dandelions saw Jen running like she had taken the object and they started to walk in her direction. Allie ran by Jen going the other way and pretended to take a handoff from her. She ran behind Mike, pretending she was carrying the remote. The Dandelions turned away from Jen and started in Allie's direction. Meanwhile, Mike fell back to the edge of the building.

Patrick slammed into a Dandelion on the right of the line. The Dandelion was a lot bigger, heavier, and stronger than Patrick. However, Patrick had caught it in the waist. This bent the Dandelion over so it could not plant its feet and Patrick was able to drive it out of the line. Nick dove through the hole Patrick had made. Meanwhile Lenore ran around the left end yelling, "I'm open. I'm open." Two confused Dandelions on the left saw Lenore and started to go after her.

Mike waited until he saw Nick turn his head. He cocked his arm and threw the remote high and long. The remote made a curved flight in the air, and as it descended, it passed just over Nick's head. He raised his hands and pulled it down and into his chest. Nick ran toward the Victory like it was the end zone on a football field. Meanwhile, Patrick continued to drive the helpless Dandelion out of its position in the line. Jen ran through the same hole as Nick, with Mike right after her.

Allie saw the two end Dandelions start after Lenore, leaving her another big hole. She ran around the open end and past the slow moving Dandelions. Patrick rolled to the right and broke contact with his opponent. He too, ran at full speed toward the Victory.

All six had gotten by the Dandelions, leaving the yellow figures in confused chaos. The neat line that had confronted the time crews was now a clump of lumbering yellow giants. It was clear they didn't know where the remote had gone or which one of the humans they should follow. It didn't matter. Once the crews were out of the beam they disappeared again. Some blue balls of light passed over their heads as the Dandelions fired wildly into the dark.

Patrick jumped into the Victory to join his five friends just as Nick pushed the button. "You've got 30 seconds, Jen," he said. Time craft are so fast that for them, 30 seconds is a long time. In five seconds the Victory was in the air a safe distance away. From this height the two crews had a real good view of the MacDonald Center. "Ten seconds," Nick said. Five. Two."

The bombs were placed on the sides of the smoke machine, so the blast went sideways, rather than up, blowing out the MacDonald Center walls. The roof, with no walls under it for support, hung in space for just a moment. Then, it crashed straight down. Everything in the building was crushed.

The smoke and dust took a long time to clear, but the time travelers in the Victory waited to see the results. When the MacDonald Center reappeared it was a low mound of rubble and junk. Nothing was left standing. They couldn't even tell it had been a building. It was like a huge giant had stepped on it and squeezed it flat. The two crews stared in awe at the wreckage. "Wow," Patrick said. Everyone else gazed in stunned silence.

This time, there was no jumping, yelling, and celebrating. It was as if the time travelers couldn't believe what had just happened. It had been a perfect mission. The Dandelions were now crippled and trapped. They were cut off and couldn't get any more supplies. They couldn't even return to their home world. They had used the MacDonald Center as their arsenal, and so most of their weapons were gone. Their smoke machine was gone. This meant they couldn't turn the earth's atmosphere into theirs. They would have to live in those yellow space suits.

As the crews continued to watch from the Victory Dandelions began to gather around the ruined building. The yellow figures stood and looked at the pile like they couldn't believe what had happened either.

"We have two bombs left," Nick said. "I think we should use them on that spaceship on the arrival/departure pad."

"Isn't that a bit of overkill?" Patrick asked. "We've done our job. Let's get out of here."

"No," Mike insisted. "The Dandelions are intelligent and they always find ways to stay a step ahead of us. They may figure out a way to use that ship to attack us from the air. We need to take it out while we have the chance. That will leave them helpless."

Jen made a slow pass over the arrival/departure pad. The Victory's door was open and the two remaining bombs stuck out just enough so they were balanced, waiting to be pushed. As Jen passed the time craft over the spaceship Dandelions on the ground spotted the craft's open door. They started shooting blue balls, but the Victory was beyond their weapons' range. The balls never even reached. When the craft was directly over the Dandelion craft, Mike and Nick pushed the bombs out the door. They fell and landed beside the spaceship. There was a huge **BOOM, BOOM** and two balls of flame rose into the sky. Jen flew away from the blasts, making a big loop around the arrival/departure pad. She then made a second pass over the pad to confirm the bombs had done their job. They had scored direct hits. The Dandelion space ship was destroyed. It was torn open and was lying on its side.

The next morning Patrick and Jen gathered at the butts with the two crews, with Charlie, and with the group leaders to report on the attack they had made the night before. The MacDonald Center was gone. The smoke machine and the new, more powerful weapons had gone with it. The last space craft was destroyed too. "We're on a roll," Patrick said. "We have one last job to do. I called you here to plan how to get it done. Nick, tell us what you have."

"We will have to plant bombs in Whittemore Center," Nick said. "I would rather bomb the building from the air just like we did the spaceship, because it would be a lot safer. But we can't. We used up all our tubes and we can't get any more. They're all buried under the MacDonald Center.

"I figure Mike and Allie are the best ones for this job," he continued. "They've already been in there and they know the layout. We need to accomplish two things. First, we want to knock out the heater. I'm guessing the eggs need to be kept warm or they will die. Second, we want to blow a big hole in the wall. That will let out the heat and it will let out the Dandelion atmosphere. That'll take care of the eggs and any Dandelions working in there.

"I think it should be a nighttime job. At night there won't be as many workers in the building. They may have a contingency plan for rescuing the eggs if they're in danger. Do the job at night. It will take more time to assemble the help for a rescue. Also, the night air will be cooler. I figure the cooler air will eliminate any leftover eggs. Taking out the heater and blowing a hole in the wall will wipe out the whole next generation in minutes.

"I've made up some fuses with a long delay. We'll use the Victory to drop off Mike and Allie. We'll get them out long before the bombs go off."

"Sounds like a plan to me," Patrick said. "We have the momentum and we have possession of the ball. We want to score the winning touchdown as soon as possible and get this game over. Mike, Allie, get ready to go tonight."

"We don't want to do it," Mike said.

"What?" Patrick asked with surprise and anger. "What do you mean you don't want to do it?"

"We don't want to do it," Mike replied firmly. "We think it's wrong." The rest of the group stared at Mike. Nick's mouth hung open in surprise.

"Let me see if I understand?" Patrick asked. "We've watched the Dandelions kill innocent, unarmed people. We also know they were planning on wiping out the human race. When did defending ourselves become wrong? It's pretty clear to me who the bad guys are, and it's not us. I've never seen a situation that was more justified. Remember what you said when we got here; it's us or them?"

"That was then," Mike answered. "Things have changed. We've beaten the Dandelions. We've put them in a real tough spot. They're completely cut off. They don't have many weapons. They can't change the air and heat the earth. They have to live in those space suits: forever. They're no longer conquering the earth. They're fighting to survive. We don't have to worry about them anymore. They've got far bigger problems to deal with.

"Allie and I think it's wrong to wipe out hundreds of innocent creatures that don't have to die. We don't know a lot about Dandelions. Are they born with a need to kill, or are they trained to do it? If it's something they learn, then they hatch innocent, and we can't kill them while they're still innocent. Allie and I can kill full grown Dandelions all day long. We've seen what they'll do to people. We can't kill something that may be born peaceful and is still innocent. It's what we don't know that bothers us. If there's a possibility we're making a mistake by blowing up the Whittemore Center, we can't do it. We have to give those eggs a chance to live. I think that's what Rabbi Cohen would tell us."

"You blasted S/Os," Patrick said shaking his head in anger and frustration. "Sometimes you guys think too much. This thing's pretty clear to the rest of us."

"That's why the Institute sends S/Os on missions," Mike answered. "We're supposed to think. We're supposed to be the crew's conscience."

"How about you, Allie?" Jen asked.

"I agree with Mike," Allie answered. "We can't risk killing hundreds of creatures that haven't done anything wrong. Maybe Dandelions are natural killers from birth, but maybe they're not. What if they have to be trained to kill? Then their young are innocent. We can't risk making a mistake that big." She rubbed the F branded on her face. "Your way is the Roman way. It was Demetrius' way. It's not my way. I came here determined to defeat evil. Dr. Newcomb taught us evil cannot overcome evil. Only good can do that."

"What happens if they hatch and we find out they are natural killers, not sweet little lizards?" Nick asked. "They have a new army. In fact, they have a *very big* new army. A lot of people will die because we were worried about their babies."

"What are they going to fight us with?" Allie asked. "We destroyed most of their weapons. What will they wear? We haven't found any baby-size space suits. The young Dandelions won't be able to leave the Whittemore Center. They're stuck in there.

"In fact, Mike made an important point," she continued. "The Dandelions are struggling to survive right now. If they build anything, they have to build places where they can live, places that have their atmosphere inside. I don't know how long those space suits are good for, but it can't be forever. When those eggs hatch, it will take all the energy the Dandelions have to care for the babies. Their conquering days are over. They're helpless. They could all be dying right now."

"Charlie," Patrick asked. "This is your world. What do you think?"

"I don't want to make such an important decision on my own," Charlie answered. "In New Durham we always talk things over as a community. We do what the majority wants and thinks proper. Right now, I want to talk with my group leaders. I need to know what they think."

"We've always been peaceful," the green group leader said. "I too have killed a lot of Dandelions. I didn't want to. I had to, but I didn't want to. If they had been peaceful, I would have been happy to have them living nearby. This world is big enough for both Dandelions and humans."

The red group leader spoke. "I agree. I never wanted to kill the Dandelions. I wish we could talk to them," she said.

"We saw what happened the last time we tried to talk," the white group leader argued, turning to speak to the red group leader. "I know they don't have a lot of weapons left. However, if we get close enough to talk they only need one gun to turn us into jelly."

"How would we talk to them, even if we wanted?" the blue group leader asked. "Anyone here know how to talk Dandelion? We can only say so much by gesturing with our hands."

After their discussion, the white group leader gave Charlie their consensus. "We don't know enough about them to decide anything," she said. "We don't even know if they can talk. Maybe they speak to each other in a way we don't know about. We can't make a decision knowing so little about them."

"What do you think about bombing the Whittemore Center?" Charlie asked his group leaders.

"I agree with Mike and Allie," the green leader responded. "The Dandelions are struggling to survive. They're no danger to us right now. I say we take some time to plan our next move. If they still want to fight, we'll have no choice. If we have to bomb the hatchery we can do it later. It's not going anywhere."

The other group leaders all nodded. "I think that's our answer," Charlie said to Patrick. "We want a truce. We want to take a break and see what the Dandelions are going to do. They wanted to wipe us out, but we don't feel the same way about them. I wish we could talk with them."

"I've decided," Allie announced. "Mike and I will go to the Whittemore Center tonight after all." This statement shocked everyone. "We're not taking bombs," Allie added. "We'll take in the translator helmets and hide them."

Lenore explained the translator helmets to Charlie and the group leaders. "They learn human languages," she said. "We don't know if they can figure out a reptilian language, but it's worth a try."

"Three days later Mike and I will go back and get the helmets," Allie said. "If we're lucky, maybe we will be able to talk lizard."

CHAPTER SEVENTEEN
MOTHERS KNOW BEST

Around midnight Jen and Lenore dropped off Allie and Mike outside the Whittemore Center. The two remembered how to get into the building and knew exactly where to go. They had decided to make this a night mission, figuring there would be fewer Dandelions in the arena. They were surprised at how few there were. This visit, only two Dandelions stood beside the moving rows, turning eggs.

The two reptilian creatures had no idea that two cloaked time travelers were in the huge arena with them. Mike and Allie were extra careful to be quiet as they moved. The place was so empty, every noise echoed. They placed the helmets on a shelf near the two Dandelions. They covered the helmets with the cloak cover and quietly left.

The next day the two crews met at the butts and Mike gave his report to Patrick and Nick. "It was easy," he said. "In fact, it was too easy. There were only two Dandelions in there. It was weird."

"It was so quiet in the rink we think we should check the place out again this morning," Allie said. "I suggest we fly the Victory over the Whittemore Center to see if there are more Dandelions there during the day. If there are never more than a few of them in the building talking, we're wasting our time. Lots of conversations are required to program the helmets."

Jen brought the Victory in low and slow over the Whittemore Center. The crews were pleased to see more Dandelions coming and going from the building during the day. Still, it was far from the busy place Mike and Allie had first visited. "I don't know why there are so few," Mike said. "We need to take a look around Durham for the missing Dandelions. Let's see if anything else is going on we should know about."

The Victory cruised over the empty streets and the time crews spotted only a few Dandelions below. Most were alone and didn't seem to be doing anything important. In fact, it was like they didn't have anything to do.

"There's a bunch of them over there," Lenore said, pointing to an open area. Jen set the craft down on the grass not far from the group. The cluster of Dandelions was facing in one direction and their attention was focused on something. They didn't appear to present any danger to the two crews. Curious to learn what was going on, the time travelers got out of the craft and snuck closer to the yellow figures. They were surprised to discover a row of a dozen Dandelions lying on the ground without yellow space suits. Mike and Allie had seen Dandelions out of their armor in the Whittemore Center. The others had only seen a Dandelion head when Nick had taken off its helmet. That was weeks ago. The two time crews examined the creatures they had been fighting. They had always thought of Dandelions as robot-like, yellow figures without any faces. The Dandelions on the ground were ugly, but there was no doubt they were some sort of creature.

Patrick led the group closer until they realized the Dandelions lined up on the ground were dead. "I wonder if these are the ones that got blown up with the MacDonald Center and the space craft," Jen whispered. They watched as several Dandelions in yellow space armor picked up a dead body. They placed it in a shallow pan that looked like a cross between a bathtub and a coffin.

One of the Dandelions took a place beside the dead body. It seemed to be leading the meeting. It moved its hands in patterns that could have been gestures. The cloaked time travelers were not sure if the gestures had meaning, or even if they were gestures at all. When it was done moving its hands the leader held one arm in the air and tipped its head back so it was facing the sky. It banged the other hand on its chest. The banging on the yellow armor sounded like a drum. The cluster of Dandelions did the same. They all held up a hand and looked at the sky and banged on their chests. The drumming on all those suits of armor was loud.

When the group was done a Dandelion stepped forward and handed the leader a small box. The leader opened the box and took out a weapon. The time travelers began to back up in fear. They were close enough for that weapon to drop them on the spot. Their fears were unfounded. The Dandelions were unaware the crews were standing nearby watching. Instead, the leader pointed the weapon at the body in the pan and shot it with a blue ball.

The time travelers gasped in surprise and watched the group around the body to see what they did next. The other yellow figures remained silent and did not move. In a couple of minutes the dead Dandelion's body began to melt. The time travelers knew it was turning into goo. Once the solid body had disappeared into colorless ooze, another Dandelion stepped forward. It handed the leader a round white object about the size of a soccer ball. "That looks like the eggs we saw in the Whittemore Center," Mike whispered to the other time travelers. The leader took a ladle and scooped up some of the thick liquid that had been a Dandelion body. He poured the ooze through a hole into the ball. He did that until he had scooped up all the goo. Then, he plugged the hole.

The leader gave the ball to three Dandelions who carried it a short distance away. They got down on their knees and clawed a hole in the ground. They carefully, almost reverently, placed the ball in the hole. Once again, they raised their hands and banged on their chests. When they were done they turned around and lay on their stomachs and using their feet, pushed the dirt back into the hole.

Two Dandelions picked up another body and everything started over again. The group looked at the sky. They raised their arms and banged. The leader shot the body. Then, it ladled the goo into a white ball. This time another group took the ball and buried it next to the first. They buried it in the same strange way. Then, the same thing happened a third time.

"Okay, let's go," Patrick said. Back in the Victory he asked, "Any idea what was going on?"

"It was a funeral," Allie said. "They were burying their dead. The Dandelion making the gestures was probably some sort of religious leader. When we were cadets Mike and I had to observe a lot of different burial ceremonies from earth's past. How people bury the dead tells us a lot about them. I think I understand the ideas behind the Dandelion funeral. The dead leave life the same way they came into life. They're reptiles. They start out as goo inside eggs, inside their mothers. After death they are turned back into goo and put into a casket that looks like an egg. They go back into ground just like they were eggs inside the mother."

"I've seen turtles lay eggs," Mike said. "They dig a hole for the eggs and then use their hind legs to push the dirt back into the hole to cover them."

"Weird," Nick said.

"Other peoples' ceremonies usually look bizarre to us," Allie explained. "But our ceremonies would look just as strange to them. The Dandelions would have thought it weird to see the villagers in New Durham place crosses and flowers where their loved ones died. What's important is what the ceremony does for someone. It has special meaning and can give them peace."

"Let's see if we can find where all the other Dandelions have gone," Jen said as she cruised over the city. She pointed below. "There's one going into that building. Let's see what it's doing in there." She set the Victory down next to the building. The cloaked time travelers got out of the craft and walked up to the windows and peered in. There were lots of Dandelions inside and they were all out of their space suits. Some were sitting. Others were stretched out on mats.

"They have their climate and their atmosphere in there," Lenore said. "They must have the same type of heat pump in this building as they do in the Whittemore Center.

"I think it's a dormitory," Mike said. "This is where they live. Correction. This is one of the places they live. We know there are a lot more Dandelions than just the ones we can see in there. They look like they don't have anything to do, like they are just waiting."

"That's exactly what's going on," Allie added. "They're waiting for the end. They fear we're going to attack again. They're helpless if we bomb them from the air. They're helpless if we attack with arrows. They don't have enough weapons to fight us."

"Almost makes me feel bad for them," Nick said sarcastically. Lenore elbowed him to shut up.

Three nights later Mike and Allie returned to the Whittemore Center to retrieve the translator helmets. Once again, the huge building was nearly empty and once again, only two Dandelions stood by the eggs turning them. Mike and Allie retrieved the helmets from their hiding place. Mike tucked them under his arm and started to leave, but Allie took him by the elbow. "Let's put them on and see if they work," she said. "If they're not completely programmed we may have to leave them here longer." They stepped behind the heat pump and donned the helmets. Then, they pulled their head covers over the helmets so they could listen without being seen.

They walked quietly from behind the heater and stood near the two Dandelions to listen. They heard a noise above them and looked up as a third Dandelion descended the stairs to the arena floor. "It's good to see another mother come to turn her young," one Dandelion said to the newcomer. Mike and Allie were startled to hear the voice. For the first time they were listening to a Dandelion speak. "A lot of these eggs have not been turned," the other lizard said to the recent arrival. "While I am here I try to turn more than just my own, but there are too many."

"I know, sister," the newcomer replied. "I come here to turn my young, but I always stay to turn some others as well. I don't know if it does any good. If only their mothers would come."

"Many are afraid," the first Dandelion replied. "Many have given up. They have no hope. They know we are all going to die. We will die if those creatures attack with their explosions and their flying sticks. We will die even if they do not attack. Perhaps the hopeless are right and nothing matters anymore."

"Many mothers cannot come," the first Dandelion said to the second. "Many will never come again. Many will never have eggs again."

"I know," the newcomer answered. "So many mothers died in the battle at the field. Five more did not come back when the leaders sent them to the village to test the new armor. Two days ago they buried the mothers who died at the smoke machine and the spaceship. These poor young. They will die like their mothers. Only, there will be no one to bury them."

"We have been lied to," the first Dandelion said. "Our leaders lied to us. We will all die because of their lies. So many have already died."

"When I was young we were peaceful," the second added. "We were peaceful before these new leaders took over. They were the ones who told us we were a great people. They said we needed more room to live. They insisted we were born to move out among the stars. We were born to conquer. We were born to rule other worlds. I wish we had never listened. I wish we had stayed on our own planet and lived peacefully."

"They told us the creatures on this planet were harmless animals with no value and little or no intelligence," the newcomer replied. "They said they lived in small groups and decorated themselves with flowers. They did nothing and they made nothing. The leaders said these creatures were worthless. It would be right to take their planet from them and make it a place for us."

"The leaders were so wrong. These creatures are very intelligent and very clever," the second said. "They have defeated us and we don't even know how they did it. All we know is we are trapped here. We cannot live on this planet and we cannot escape. Our leaders have killed us. They have killed our young."

"Sisters," the first Dandelion mother said after a pause, "The leaders don't control us anymore. They are on our home planet. They cannot come here anymore than we can go back there. So, no one has any authority now. When I am done turning my eggs and some of the others, I know what I am going to do. I am going to the creatures who own this world. We have learned they are intelligent. In fact, they may be more intelligent than we are. I will try to find a way to talk to them. If I do, I will ask them not to kill us. I will ask them to leave us in peace. I will ask them to let us die peacefully, or to let us find a way to survive. Maybe there are mothers among them. Maybe their mothers will listen to another mother."

Jen and Lenore returned Mike and Allie to the village with the programmed helmets. The next morning they gave the helmets to Charlie and the group leaders. "You'll be wearing these from now on," Mike told Charlie. "It's not our job to work out your future. Nick, will you show Charlie how the helmets work?"

While Charlie was trying on the helmet the alarm bell began to ring. Menlo knew this meant danger and he took off in the direction of the field baying loudly, his fishhook tail straight up in the air. Charlie and the time crews ran after Menlo, following him to the field. The archers grabbed their bows. Their quivers were full of both bodkin points and explosive arrows. They followed their group leaders and fell into a battle line at the edge of the field.

On the other side of the open expanse three yellow figures were starting the long walk across. Patrick studied them with his binoculars. "I don't see any weapons," he said. "They look unarmed. Why are they walking like that?"

The other time travelers examined the Dandelions with their binoculars. "They're walking with their arms held out," Allie said. "They're using the same gestures the village leaders did when they were gunned down. They're copying the village leaders. They're trying to say they come in peace. They want to talk." Turning to Mike she added,

"You and I know who those three Dandelions are."

"I'm going out to meet them," Charlie said with determination.

"Put on a helmet," Nick told Charlie.

The man began to walk across the field toward the three Dandelions. His wife held their child and watched. Charlie held up his arms in the same gesture of peace. When he met the group of Dandelions he stopped. He was too far away for the time travelers or the villagers to hear what he was saying.

"Guys," Patrick said to the time crews. "What happens from now on is not our business and we can't get involved. New Durham and the Dandelions have to work out their own futures. With everyone focused on Charlie, this is a good time for us to return where we belong."

The two time crews and Menlo walked back to the village and to the Victory.

CHAPTER EIGHTEEN
VICTORY'S FATE

Jen landed the Victory behind the crew apartment building and cloaked it. It was afternoon when the time travelers arrived back at their quarters and all six relaxed in the boy's living room. "Well, I think that was a winner," Patrick said with satisfaction. "Humanity goes on living peacefully. It has a good future, even though it will never time travel again."

"They had stopped doing that anyway," Nick added. "It was a small price to pay for a peaceful future. The only question is the Dandelions. Did they make it or not? I'll bet the humans help them and they live peacefully side by side," he said, answering his own question. Nick was pretty proud of the part he had played in this mission.

"I'm not as sure as you guys," Mike added. Nick and Patrick looked at Mike like he had rained on their parade.

"Okay, Egghead," Patrick said with his usual annoyance. "What are you getting at?"

"We know humans have a long and bloody history," Mike explained. "As soon as we learned to throw rocks we started fighting and killing each other. It didn't change until after the Hampton Summit. Think about what we did to the people in New Durham. We gave weapons to those peaceful villagers. We taught them how to make bows and arrows and gunpowder and bombs. We taught them how to use those weapons to kill. History teaches they are more likely to turn those weapons on each other than to go back to living peacefully.

"Once they start fighting, they will develop better and better weapons," he continued. "It will be like the Dandelions and us. One side will try to get a step ahead of the other, to get an advantage. There will be an arms race and lots of bloody wars."

"Well, you just ruined it for me," Patrick said in disgust. He got up to go to the refrigerator. "Anyone want something to drink?" he asked, trying to change the subject.

"We had to do it," Nick argued to Mike. "Those people would have all been killed if we hadn't shown them how to defend themselves."

"Right," Mike answered. "I'm not saying we were wrong. I agree we did what we had to do. For humanity, it was life or death. I'm saying I don't know what the future will be for those people. Humanity has a bad track record."

"We'll have to trust Charlie," Jen said. "We taught him to be a leader. Let's hope he's a good one."

"We do have to make a promise to each other," Allie said. "We can never tell anyone else what we saw. If we do, we risk changing time. People will try to prevent the Dandelions from coming through the wormhole. They will make sure that humans don't stop time traveling and don't become Hippies."

"I really wish we could talk to Dr. Newcomb and Rabbi Cohen," Mike said.

"We can't," Allie said forcefully. "We know Dr. Newcomb keeps a diary. We know Charlie's family has that diary. We can't risk Dr. Newcomb writing about what we did. That would change history. We have to promise never to talk to anyone other than ourselves. We can't tell our parents. We can't keep diaries. When we get older we can't tell the people we marry. We can't tell our children. It has to be our secret – as long as we live. "

"We still have to take care of one last detail," Jen added. "We have a cloaked time craft behind this building. We have to find a better place to hide it."

"We should destroy it," Mike said.

Once again Patrick got angry. "Why?" he demanded. "That is a perfectly good time craft. You S/Os get under my skin."

"We have to destroy it precisely because it is a perfectly good time craft," Mike answered. "That's part of the problem. There's another part. Its frame of origination is in the far future. Anyone who gets his hands on that craft can go both forward and back in time. They can go as far forward as New Durham. No matter how careful we are to keep our secret someone else can learn it by using the Victory. They can change history."

"Sometimes I hate S/Os," Patrick said angrily. "How come nothing is ever simple for you? It is for the rest of us."

"Remember," Allie added. "Time travel messes with your mind. Right now, it's messing with your thinking, Patrick. Even after we die, the Victory will still be able to go forward in time. We may keep our secret all our lives. We may not leave behind diaries. But, we will leave the Victory behind. When we're gone we'll have no control over what anyone does with it. I agree with Mike. We need to destroy it."

By now, Patrick was really unhappy. "No," he insisted. "No. I will not let that happen. I *will not* let that happen."

"We can't take the chance, Patrick," Mike insisted.

"You're not a pilot," Patrick shot back. "You don't know what a craft means to me and Jen. You don't destroy a craft."

"Let's take a lesson from the villagers at New Durham," Jen said, trying to stop the feud between her fellow pilot and his S/O. "They solved everything by majority. Let's take a vote. Do we keep the Victory?"

Jen, Patrick, Nick, and Lenore raised their hands. "That settles it," Mike said. "I'll go along with the majority, even if I think you're wrong."

"Me too," Allie added with a shrug of her shoulders. "Now that we've made that decision we're back to Jen's question. What do we do with the Victory? We can't leave it behind the crew quarters. We can't take it to the hanger."

"It will be safe with the CT 9225," Patrick said. "We should leave it in the woods behind Mike's house. We know that no one ever goes into those woods. It will be safe as long as Mike lives there. After that, we'll have to find another spot.

"Jen," he said. "We still have time this afternoon to take it back to my time. If you and Lenore fly the Victory, Nick and I will follow in the CT 9225. We'll bring you back. We'll return in time for supper together.

"Will you two eggheads be okay if we leave you alone for a while?" Patrick asked Mike and Allie. "You won't come up with anymore crazy ideas?" The two S/Os knew he wasn't angry anymore and that he was making peace with them.

"We'll have supper ready," Allie said reassuringly to show she held no hard feelings. "Don't be late or you'll eat cold food."

After supper Lenore excused herself. "I have to be back in class tomorrow morning," she said.

"We have to make our report to Prof. Garcia on longbows and Agincourt," Mike added.

"We also have to start teaching," Nick said. "I'll see you in my class," he said to Lenore. "Sorry I have to treat you like everyone else," he teased.

"You guys will be here two more weeks while you teach," Jen said. "When will you go back?"

I'm in no hurry," Patrick said. "I could live here all the time and be real happy. I guess I'd miss my family," he added.

"I graduate in three weeks," Lenore added. "Could you guys stay that long? I'd love to have you attend."

"I'm up for it," Mike answered as he put his arm around Allie's shoulder. "That gives me plenty of time to write my paper on life during the Civil War. I won't be under any pressure to get it done over the weekend."

The five young time travelers found their seats for the cadet graduation ceremony. Mike had Menlo on a leash. Graduation took place outdoors on the arrival/departure pad. The group looked around at this familiar location. The last time they had seen this area it was overgrown with weeds and bushes. The hanger was run down and the door at the end was hanging off its hinges. The Dandelion space ship was blown open and lying on its side, not far from where they sat.

Today, the pad and hanger were spotless. They had been cleaned and decorated for the graduation. A long row of time craft was parked in front the hanger. All the time crews had returned from their missions to attend. No matter how young or old a time traveler may be, each had graduated from this same school, at this same spot. They had come back to see the next class graduate. In a couple of days the cadets in that class would receive their assignments and would join the older crews in their work.

The Smith family had reserved seats for the two time crews and Mr. Smith greeted the Fixer team. The boys were surprised to see he was wearing an Atlantic Academy baseball cap. Mr. Smith saw the boys stare at the cap and smiled as he took it off. "When you have no hair, you need to protect your head from the sun," he said with a laugh. The boys laughed too as they saw the bright light gleam off the shiny, dark brown skin on the top of Mr. Smith's head.

Mrs. Smith was as nice as the last time the boys had seen her. Mr. Smith introduced Jen and Allie to his wife. "We're so happy that Lenore will be the engineer on the Auckland," Mrs. Smith said. "We're very happy that she will be your roommate at the crew quarters. You'll see us when we come by to visit her. I'll make sure you three always have plenty of cookies."

"This is Charmaine Jackson," Mr. Smith said to the crews. "Charmaine is living with us until next term when she becomes a cadet at the Institute." He placed his hand on Charmaine's shoulder. The girl's skin was the color of coffee and cream. She had greenish brown eyes and a round, wide nose. Her medium brown hair was wild and bushy. To keep it under control she tied it back with a scrunchy. She was shy and quiet. The boys all shook her hand and congratulated her on being accepted as a cadet. The girl left to take her seat.

"Charmaine is an orphan," Mr. Smith explained. "Her parents were part of a time crew and were close friends of ours. They died in a time craft accident at Roswell, New Mexico. Charmaine has no other family, so she's living with us until next term. She and Lenore are nearly the same age and have always been like sisters. We're proud that she is becoming a cadet. Like us, time travel is her family business," he added with a smile.

After graduation Lenore found her family. Everyone congratulated her and hugged her. When it was Allie's turn Lenore looked at her cheek. "Allie, your scar. It's gone," she said.

Allie touched her cheek. It was as smooth as the other. "I kept the scar to remind myself that evil is real," she said. "In the Roman Empire I only saw evil win, over and over. I needed to know that evil could lose. I had to keep the scar until I saw it beaten. I witnessed that in New Durham. I helped defeat evil and I didn't need the scar anymore. Last week, I had the doctors fix my cheek. I'll tell you more back at our quarters when we can talk."

At the end of several weeks, the three Fixers had to go back to Atlantic Academy. The boys and the Auckland's crew walked down to the arrival/departure pad. There, the two crews hugged goodbye. The hugs were long and involved lots of kisses. Menlo saw everyone hugging and wanted to get in on it. He jumped up on Mike and Allie and kissed them on the face. Then, he moved onto Jen and Patrick. Finally, he lapped Nick and Lenore as they were trying to kiss goodbye. Nick was so tall he had to bend over to hug Lenore. "That was a wet kiss, Menlo" Nick said as he wiped his cheek. The dog circled the couples wagging his J-shaped tail vigorously.

Patrick set the CT 9225 down behind Mike's home. Mike took Menlo inside the house and left him. The next landing was on Atlantic Academy's roof. The three boys changed back into their school uniforms and stored their gray Fixer uniforms in a cupboard under one of the CT 9225's seating platforms. They descended the staircase that led to the roof. At the bottom, they opened the door into the corridor just a crack, to be sure the coast was clear. No one was there. The last class of the day was still in session. The boys were walking down the corridor when the bell rang. The classroom doors opened and the students filed out.

Patrick, Nick, and Mike walked across the parking lot together. "See you guys on Monday," Patrick said as they split up to go to their family cars.

Mike climbed into his mother's station wagon. Menlo was in the back seat. The dog put his head over the seat and kissed Mike. "Hi, Mennie," Mike said. "Did you have a nice day?"

Mike kissed his mother on the cheek. "Did you have a nice day?" Mrs. Castleton asked.

"Yeah. It was good. Pretty much like any other day," Mike said. "What are we doing tonight?"

"Your father's on another science fiction kick," Mrs. Castleton answered. "He rented a classic science fiction movie for us to watch. It's another story by H. G. Wells."

"Great," Mike replied. "I like those classic movies. Which one is it?"

Mrs. Castleton was ready to back out of the parking spot and looked in the mirror to make sure there were no children behind her. She answered, *"War of the Worlds."*

ABOUT THE AUTHOR

Mike Dunbar began writing as a 19-year old cub reporter. Since then, he has published seven books on wood crafting and written more magazine articles than he can remember. His name has been on the mastheads of three national magazines. He has been a newspaper and magazine columnist, and an editor. He has hosted a radio and a television show. He is in demand as a seminar speaker. He lives in Hampton, NH with his family. He operates and teaches at The Windsor Institute, a school that specializes in handmade Windsor chairs, and blogs at mikedunbar.tumblr.com, windsorchairs.tumblr.com, and thewindsorinstitute.com/blog. The Castleton Series is his first fiction writing, and he is pleased to present book three, The End of Time, to the world.

SAMPLE OF BOOK FOUR IN THE CASTLETON SERIES AVAILABLE FOR SALE JANUARY, 2014

Chapter One
Flight 19

Lieutenant Chuck Newcomb entered the door of the officers club at Naval Air Station Fort Lauderdale. The 25 year old Navy pilot had just eaten lunch and planned to finish it off with some coffee. He walked to a table and poured himself a cup. Next, the tall, thin pilot picked up a red crayon and drew a dark red line through the date on the calendar – December 5, 1945. He sat down in an upholstered arm chair and took a long sip of his coffee. "One less day before you become a free man," said Lieutenant Charlie Taylor, sitting in the next chair. Like Chuck, Lt. Taylor was wearing tan slacks and a tan, short-sleeved shirt. This was the uniform Navy officers wore when they were on duty.

"Yup," replied Lt. Newcomb. "Less than six months now. I can't wait for May 1 when my enlistment is up and I say goodbye to the Navy. I should be able to get back home to Baltimore before my wife has the baby. This is our first and I want to be there with her."

"You'll miss flying," said Lt. Taylor, teasing his friend. "You'll miss Navy food and Navy coffee."

"Not much," Lt. Newcomb answered. "My wife's a great cook and she makes much better coffee. As for flying, I'm going to apply for a job with

TransAmerican Airlines. Now that the war is over they're buying old Army and Navy DC 3s. They're turning those military gooney birds into passenger planes. The company figures they can sell plane tickets as cheap as the trains, and get people where they're going a lot faster. I think they're right. Flying will be the way people travel in the future. I want to get in on the ground floor."

"There are gonna be a lot of military pilots looking for jobs," Lt. Taylor replied. "Jobs flying passenger planes are gonna be hard to get."

"I'm figuring I have a leg up," Lt. Newcomb said. "I teach flying. After all those missions I flew during the war the Navy made me a trainer. You know, you're a trainer too. You should think about flying passenger planes, Taylor. TransAm pilots make good money."

"We teach pilots to fly Avenger bombers," Lt. Taylor argued. "We dive straight down until we almost crash into a ship. We drop a bomb and then fly straight up again. We'd have more luck getting a job running a roller coaster. TransAmerican doesn't want the kind of flying we do."

"Suit yourself," Lt. Newcomb answered. "I'm applying for the job. Don't come knockin' on my door lookin' for a loan when I'm a rich, successful airline pilot." The two flyers laughed.

"Can I get you to do me a favor, Chuck?" Lt. Taylor asked after a short pause.

"Sure," Lt. Newcomb answered. "What is it?"

"I'm supposed to take up Flight 19 and test them on Navigation Problem Number One," Lt. Taylor said. "You know, I gotta watch a bunch of trainees take a combination of bombing and navigation tests. I had a late night and I'm dead tired. Would you take my place? It's a piece of cake. These guys have a lot of experience and a trainee will lead the flight. You just have to watch 'em and make sure they don't get lost."

"Can't help you out, Buddy," Lt. Newcomb said, slowly shaking his head. "You're scheduled for Flight 19 at 1:45. I take up Flight 23 at 4:00 for the same test. If I fly your mission, I won't be back in time for mine."

"Guess I'd better have another cup of coffee," Lt. Taylor said with resignation. "That's the only way I'll stay awake. From now on I gotta get to bed earlier. Well, I better get to the ready room or I'll be late for the flight."

Lt. Newcomb relaxed in his chair as his friend stood up and poured himself a cup of coffee. Lt. Taylor put on his officer's cap and left the officers club, coffee in hand.

Lt. Newcomb still had a couple of hours of free time. He took out his wallet and opened it to a picture of his wife. He gazed lovingly at her. He kissed the picture and returned the wallet to his pocket. He put his head back on the chair and soon, he was asleep.

In his dreams he was back at his home in Baltimore. He was playing ball with his young son. The baby would not be born for six months and could just as well turn out to be a girl. However, in Chuck's dream it was the son he wanted so badly. He named the boy Charles, just like his father and grandfather. However, in his dream he called the boy Junior. He could tell from the way the boy threw the ball, Junior Newcomb was a natural athlete, a natural ball player. He would be a pitcher. There was no doubt he would play in the major leagues - for the Baltimore Orioles. He would lead his team to the World Series and win the final game with his brilliant pitching.

"Lieutenant! Lieutenant Newcomb," a far away voice called urgently. "Lieutenant, Sir. Wake up." Chuck Newcomb opened his eyes. He was surprised to see a sailor standing in front of his chair. The only enlisted men allowed in the club were those that worked there. They were cooks and waiters and they all wore white jackets. Standing in front of him was an enlisted man, dressed in a pale blue denim shirt and dark denim work pants. What was an ordinary sailor dressed in work clothes doing in the officers club? Chuck wiped the sleep from his eyes.

"Lieutenant Newcomb, Sir," the sailor said. "Lieutenant, they want you at the tower. Right away, Sir."

"Why," Lieutenant Newcomb asked as the last images of his dream disappeared like smoke. "What's the matter?"

"It's Lieutenant Taylor, Sir," the sailor said. "It's Flight 19. They're in trouble. You gotta get to the tower right away, Sir. This is an emergency."

Lt. Newcomb grabbed his officer cap and ran out the door. He was tall, thin and had long legs, so was able to run much faster than the sailor. When he reached the tower he ran up the stairs taking two steps at a time. He burst open the tower door. "What's happened to Lt. Taylor?" he demanded.

"Listen, Sir," the radio operator said.

Lt. Taylor's voice came from the speaker. "I don't know where we are," he said. "Fort Lauderdale. Can you see us on radar? Where are we?"

Another officer named Lt. Bob Fox was also in the tower listening to the messages from Flight 19. "One of my students received a transmission, Chuck," Lt. Fox said to Lt. Newcomb. "I was taking up Flight 20. We were ready to take off to do Navigation Problem Number One. A voice on the radio asked my student what his compass reading was. We didn't know if the message was coming from a boat or a plane. We asked the caller to identify himself. He said his name was Powers and he was with Flight 19.

"A while later we heard another call. This one was Lt. Taylor. He said both of his compasses were out and he was trying to find Fort Lauderdale, Florida. He said he was over land but it was broken patches, like islands. He thought he was in the Keys, but he didn't know how far down. He asked how to get to Fort Lauderdale. I came up here to the tower to report what we had heard. The tower had gotten the same messages."

Now, things got really crazy. Taylor's voice came over the radio. "Fort

Lauderdale. My instruments are spinning."

Chuck Newcomb took the radio microphone. "Taylor," he said. "This is Chuck. Forget your instruments. It's afternoon. The sun is in the west. Turn the planes so you are facing it. That will bring you back to land."

"I can't see the sun," Lt. Taylor answered. He sounded scared. "It's like we're in a cloud. I can't see anything. I can see the other planes as clear as day. So, I know we're not in a cloud. I just can't tell where the light's coming from. Everything else has disappeared. I don't know how to find up or down. Without instruments I'm afraid we're gonna crash into the sea. We don't know where the sea is."

Chuck Newcomb turned to the sailor who had awakened him in the officer's club. "Get down to the hanger," he said. "Have the crew get my plane ready. Find Ensign Dubois. Tell him he's flying with me as my radioman." He turned to Lt. Fox and said, "I'm going out to find Taylor and his flight. I need you to stay here in the tower and keep in radio contact with me. Let me know if you receive any more messages and tell me what they are.

"Taylor's a good pilot," Lt. Newcomb continued. "He and his flight are close to where they should be. It just sounds like his instruments have stopped working. If you stay here and keep in touch with me on the radio," Lt. Newcomb said as ran out the door, "you should be able to lead me right to him." On the way down he again took the stairs two at a time. He was running across the runway when Lt. Fox yelled down to him from the tower. "Why aren't the instruments working in the other planes?" Lt. Newcomb was too far away to hear.

Chuck ran into the ready room. There he put on his pilot's coveralls and pulled a tight fitting leather helmet over his head. The helmet had a radio speaker over one ear so he could hear radio messages. He strapped on his bright yellow, inflatable life preserver and grabbed his parachute. He threw the parachute over his shoulder so it looked like a back pack. He was half way out the door when he turned and went back to his locker. He took his pistol out of the metal cabinet and strapped it on his hip. He patted the gun like it gave him a sense of security. He didn't know why he would need a pistol, but going into a strange situation he just felt better with it.

Strapped into his plane's cockpit Lt. Newcomb used the plane's intercom to ask Ensign Dubois if he was ready for takeoff. The radioman's seat faced the plane's tail. In combat, he would have a machine gun to protect the plane from an enemy approaching from behind. However, this plane was a trainer and was unarmed. Chuck Newcomb gave a thumb up to the men on the runway to tell them he was ready to go. He began his taxi out to the end of the runway.

When he was in place for takeoff he gave his huge engine the gas. The engine roared and the propeller became a spinning blur. The big Avenger bomber started down the runway, rapidly gaining speed. Soon, the wheels left the ground and Chuck Newcomb pulled the plane's nose skyward to gain altitude. Then, he turned the plane eastward over the Atlantic Ocean and towards Hens and Chickens Shoals. Those were the tiny islands where the Navy practiced bombing. "He's still in that area," Lt. Newcomb said to Ensign Dubois, who was sitting behind him. "We'll be there in a half hour. We'll have Flight 19 back on the ground in time for supper."

"Chuck," a voice said over the radio. It was Lt. Fox. "We heard from Taylor again. He's still lost and says he can't see anything. I told him you were on the way. I told him to fly in circles. That way he stays in the area where he is."

"Good idea," Lt. Newcomb radioed back. "I don't need him flying off looking for land. I'll just end up in a wild goose chase. I'm going to fly zigzag through the area around Hens and Chickens. That way, if he's flying circles, we'll run into each other."

At that moment Lt. Newcomb heard a message on his radio from Taylor. "This is crazy," the frightened voice said. "Everything's crazy. What's going on? This can't be." Taylor sounded like he was about to break down from fear.

"Charlie," Chuck Newcomb called over his plane's radio to Taylor. "Charlie. Hold on. I'm almost there. Just keep flying in circles. I'll find you and lead you back." In five minutes Chuck Newcomb saw the small islands called Hens and Chickens. "Charlie, I'm here," he radioed. There was silence. "Charlie. Lt. Taylor. Flight 19. We've arrived. Talk to me. Someone talk to me." The radio remained silent.

"Ft. Lauderdale," Chuck Newcomb radioed. "Bob. Have you heard from Taylor?"

"No," Bob Fox's voice answered. "He hasn't radioed for 10 minutes. He sounded scared. We heard him say everything was crazy. He sounded like he was going crazy."

"If he didn't report he was going down I'm gonna guess he's still up here," Chuck replied. "Maybe his radio broke down too."

"Why aren't the other planes radioing, Chuck?" Bob Fox asked. "All their compasses and radios can't be broke. Why didn't the other planes lead Taylor back?"

"I don't know," Chuck replied. That was the first time he had thought about that question. Bob was right. All their instruments couldn't break down at the same time. That was crazy. Lt. Newcomb began to fly a pattern of zigzags over the small islands. He went west for a while, flying away from land. He then turned around to fly back east toward land. Each time, he moved a little more north. This way, he would eventually cover the entire area, and he would find Taylor. When he did, he would signal Flight 19 to follow him back to Naval Air Station Ft. Lauderdale and to safety.

Lt. Newcomb squinted as he scanned the sky in front of his plane. He turned his head and scanned the sky side-to-side. Meanwhile, Ensign Dubois scanned the sky behind the plane, as well as looking side-to-side. Between the pilot and the radio man, they could see the entire sky around the Avenger.

Other than Lt. Taylor, they didn't know the other flyers in those missing planes. Those were younger men learning to be bomber crews. However, Newcomb and Dubois had just finished fighting World War II and they had known hundreds of other flyers. Flyers were all like brothers. They took care of each other. Somewhere out there were five missing planes and 10 of their brothers. They knew that if they were the ones who were lost, each of those missing flyers would volunteer for the rescue mission.

Back at Naval Air Station Fort Lauderdale the radar man was watching Lt. Newcomb's plane on his radar screen. It appeared as a green blip. Suddenly, three more blips appeared right behind Lt. Newcomb. "Lt. Fox," the radar man said. "I think Lt. Newcomb has found some of Flight 19. Look here." He showed Lt. Fox the three new blips.

"Chuck," Lt. Fox said into the radio microphone. "Chuck. You're in luck. They found you. You have three planes on your tail. Can you identify them? Is Taylor one of them?"

"You see any planes behind us, Dubois?" Lt. Newcomb asked his radioman.

"Nothing there, Sir," Dubois answered.

"No planes behind us, Bob," Lt. Newcomb radioed back to Ft. Lauderdale.

Bob Fox and the radar man continued to stare at the blips. "They're right behind you, Chuck," he said. "If they were enemy planes they could shoot you out of the sky, they're so close."

"Nothing there," answered Lt. Newcomb's voice. "Dubois has a clear view behind the plane. There's nothing there. Maybe they're just ghost images."

"Sir," the radar man said to Lt. Fox. "I ran radar through the whole war. I know radar inside and out. Those are not ghost images, Sir. Those are craft. I don't know how Ensign Dubois can miss them. They're right in his face. If they got any closer they'd bump the plane."

"Taylor," Lt. Fox said into the radio microphone. "Do you see Lt. Newcomb's plane ahead of you?" There was no answer. "Any plane in Flight 19," he said. "Report. Do you see an Avenger just ahead of you?" Silence.

"Unidentified aircraft,'" Lt. Fox said into the radio. "You are in restricted air space. Identify yourself." There was no answer.

Chuck was scanning the sky straight ahead of the plane when he noticed his compass needle swing. It went to the right and then to the left. Then, it returned to its original position. Chuck ignored it. He was busy searching the sky. Five minutes later Ensign Dubois said, "Darned thing." He banged on his radio.

"What's up," Chuck asked.

"My radio just changed frequency. I'm not in touch with Ft. Lauderdale anymore. I'll adjust it. Ft. Lauderdale, do you read me?"

"Copy," said a voice, but it was very faint and nearly covered by static.

At that point Chuck Newcomb saw his compass needle swing again. This time it did not stop. In fact, it began to spin. He looked at the altimeter, a device that told the pilot how high he was. The altimeter is a very important instrument. In rain or fog a plane could fly into the ground without the pilot knowing he was too low. Like the compass, the Avenger's altimeter began to swing. "What's going on?" Lt. Newcomb asked out loud.

"Chuck," Ensign Dubois said. "Look at the sky. It's weird."

Ensign Dubois was right. Everything was gone. There were no clouds. There was no sun. He couldn't see the ocean, and he couldn't see the sky. Everything was gray. There was light, so Lt. Newcomb could see. There just wasn't anything to see. He held up his hand. It did not make a shadow. The light was not coming from anywhere, but it was everywhere. "I don't know what's happened, Dubois. I'm going to turn around and see if we can fly back out of this."

Chuck quickly realized that without instruments or anything to see, he wouldn't know when he had turned his plane around. He could go in a complete circle. He guessed and then, looked at his watch so he would know how long he flew in the new direction. His watch said 12:00. He knew it was about 4:00. "What time is it, Dubois," he asked his radioman.

"My watch is on the fritz," Dubois answered. "It says its 12:00. The second hand is on the 12 too. It's not moving."

"Tell Ft. Lauderdale we're having trouble," Lt. Newcomb told his radioman.

"Naval Air Station Ft. Lauderdale," Dubois said into his microphone. "This is TB Avenger 307. Ensign Dubois speaking. Ft. Lauderdale, we're having trouble. Our instruments are not working. Do you read me?"

"TB Avenger 307. I read you," said the voice. "What's your position?"

"We don't know," Dubois answered. "We were over the Hens and Chickens, but now we can't see anything."

"You must be over a cloud," the voice said. "Where's the sun?"

"There is no sun," Dubois answered. He realized he had just repeated almost word for word what Taylor had said, and realized he had the same fear in his own voice. "There is no nothing."

The voice replied, "Look for anything...." It stopped in the middle of the word. The tower at Fort Lauderdale was gone. Within seconds the Avenger's engine began to sputter. It was shutting down. Chuck Newcomb tried to start it again. Nothing happened. Nothing in the plane worked. It was like all the electricity was gone.

"We're gonna have to bailout, Dubois," Newcomb yelled to his radioman. "I'll try to keep us gliding. Open the canopy." Dubois undid his safety harness and turned so he could reach forward. He unlocked the canopy, the curved windshield that covers the cockpit, and slid it back out of the way. Now, he and the pilot could climb up and jump away from the plane so they were not hurt, or get their parachutes tangled in the tail.

Standing with his head above the canopy Dubois said to the pilot, "There's no wind." The plane was moving so fast through the air that wind should be blowing on him like a hurricane. It was not. The air was calm.

"Don't be crazy," Chuck Newcomb answered. "If we weren't moving through the air, we would fall out of the sky. There has to be wind." He held his hand above the canopy, but he too could feel no wind. "What? How are we staying in the air?"

"Maybe we're not," Dubois answered. He climbed out of the cockpit and stepped carefully onto the wing. Still no wind, no vibration. It was like the plane was parked on the runway at Ft. Lauderdale. Dubois got on his stomach and looked under the wing. He could see nothing. He held on to the edge of the wing and slowly lowered himself down. When his feet reached the bottom of the plane he felt something hard, and tested his footing. He could stand. He took a step very carefully because he could not see any surface under his feet. He could only feel it, and didn't know where it might end. He was afraid he could step off an edge and fall. He took several more steps, still being very careful, but there were no problems.

"It's okay, Lieutenant," Ensign Dubois said to the pilot. Chuck Newcomb climbed out of the cockpit, climbed down off the wing, and walked until he stood beside the radioman. Together, they walked a short distance in front of the plane. When they turned to look back at the plane, it was gone. They looked around for it. When Ensign Dubois again spotted the plane it appeared to be below them. The plane was on its side. Well, it was not lying on its side, that's just how they saw the plane. They were not looking down on the cockpit like they would if they were above their craft. It was like they were standing beside the plane looking at it, but it was under them. Ensign Dubois took ahold of the strap on Lt. Newcomb's parachute. It was like he was afraid of loosing his pilot.

"Look!" Chuck Newcomb said with so much surprise he almost yelled to the radioman. In front of them was a crew member from Flight 19. At least it looked like it could be a Navy flyer. The man was flat. He looked like a guy in a cartoon who gets run over by a steam roller and is pressed flat like a pancake. At first, Newcomb and Dubois thought the guy was dead, but there was no blood. Then, they saw the guy's mouth and eyes move. Next, he seemed to wave his arm. It looked like he was talking.

With Ensign Dubois still holding Lt. Newcomb's parachute, they stepped toward the man, but they were held back by an invisible cord, or a string. They heard a voice say, "Hey, that hurts. Who's pushing me?' The voice was Lt. Taylor's.

"Taylor," Chuck said pushing again on the invisible string. "Taylor. Where are you?"

"Right here," Taylor answered. "What the heck's pushing me? It hurts."

Another voice said, "This can't be. This can't be."

"That's right," Dubois said to Newcomb, holding even tighter to the strap. "This can't be. This is all impossible."

OTHER BOOKS BY SOUL STAR

The Price of Honor by Gus Gallows

Ganth, the Minotaur Empire, stretching across the continent of Ice Wall within the realm of Algoron, is a place where Honor is the foremost trait among its citizens. Here strength defines law; a law that has left Pah'min in disgrace. His life in Ganth forfeit, his childhood love denied; he is snubbed by all. But there is one House that will accept him. The secret house is despised as an honor-lacking abode of spies. It is from this dark place that Pah'min must begin the long and painful trek to restore his honor. He must begin again in the land of his enemies, and feign loyalty to a king he loathes. There will be many foes on all sides, but his greatest battles are within as the gods themselves try to sway him toward their own mysterious end. Ultimately, he must escape, sacrificing those he holds dear, all to pay the price... The Price of Honor.

Available in e-book format through Smashwords
https://www.smashwords.com/books/view/345472 or your local e-book retailer. Available in paperback through createspace https://www.createspace.com/4394101 or order through your local book store.

The Lost Crew by Mike Dunbar

In book two of the Castleton series Allie, Jen, and their comrade Bashir are sent on a mission to study the roots of Jazz. They follow this music back through time -- from New Orleans, to Paris, and to ancient Carthage. Unbeknownst to the Time Institute the crew are captured and sold into the Roman Empire as slaves. Mike, Nick, and Patrick are recruited for their first rescue mission. They must retrace the lost crew's steps, discover what happened, and bring their fellow time travelers home. By the time they arrive will their friends be alive or dead? Can they be saved without changing time and setting off Chaos? Do their friends want to be saved? You'll discover once again that time travel messes with your mind and with your heart.

Available in paperback through
Createspace http://bit.ly/1e6FwKi or your local book dealer.

Available in e-book through Smashwords http://bit.ly/18Ntk45

Elements of a Broken Mind By Heidi Angell

Grant Anderson is a small-town detective whose job was quiet and easy, until three girls end up dead. A serial killer is stalking the young ladies in his town. Without the high tech equipment of big cities at his fingers, Grant must rely on good old-fashioned police work; but with no discernible pattern and no clues to follow, the case seems to be grinding to a halt.

Then Grant gets a visit from a mysterious young woman. Who is Clear Angel? What is her connection to the case? If Grant is to believer her, then he must accept that she has "seen" these things. But Grant is a professional. He cannot believe in psychics! Yet when another girl goes missing, and Grant's search is yielding nothing he is desperate enough to try.

Grant and Clear team up to stop a madman bent on the destruction of the world. As their feelings for one another grow, they try to deny them. But when Clear goes missing, Grant must face his feelings and save her before it is too late.

Available in Paperback through
Createspace<u>https://www.createspace.com/4302361</u> or your

local store.

Available in e-book through
Smashwords<u>https://www.smashwords.com/books/view/325771</u>

The Hampton Summit by Mike Dunbar

Time travel messes with your mind, and your love life. That's what you'll discover in the Castleton Series, an eight-book romantic/adventure saga for smart, curious readers. The series leads you back to the dawn of humanity, into the distant future, and ends up where it began - messing with your mind all the way. The Castleton Series is the story of young teens Mike Castleton and Allie Tymoshenko. The pair fall in love, but they are star-crossed, having been born seven generations apart. When Allie meets the boy from the past, she recognizes him as the young Captain Mike Castleton of the band the Sirens. When older, Mike will set off a revolution in music known as Chamber Rock. Allie can never tell Mike about his future, and the mystery surrounding Captain Mike; at the peak of his career, he disappears. In this series you will follow the lovers as they age and mature, and search for happiness. The series will mess with your mind as the couple experiences amazing and dangerous adventures in time. In this first book The Hampton Summit, Allie and Mike meet when Mike and his friends are recruited by time travelers to prevent a murder in their hometown. A team of renegades from the Time Institute intends to kill a wheelchair-bound scientist before he can share a discovery that creates the peaceful future Allie knows. The assassins' goal is to rearrange the past so they can dominate the chaotic world they create. Traveling forward in time to be trained at the Institute, the boys are befriended by fellow cadets,

Allie, and her roommate, Jen. Using only their wits, the group of innovative and resourceful teens risks their own lives as they take on the team of killers. In the process, Mike and Allie kindle a romance that can never be.

Available in Paperback from your local book dealer or Createspace https://www.createspace.com/4201346

In E-book formats through Smashwords

https://www.smashwords.com/books/view/296925

The Hunters by Heidi Angell

What would you do if you found your town had been infested with vampires? For Chris and his brother Lucas, the answer was simple enough: you fight back. Gathering a small band of other people in their town who have been affected by the vampires, they begin a resistance. But after a year of fighting, they have only managed to kill a handful, while the vampire leader has turned five times that many.

Then two enigmatic strangers appear, changing the groups lives even further.

Fury and Havoc. They call themselves hunters, and want no part in this little band of heroes. Ordering them to lay low, the duo vow to rid their town of vampires. When Fury is injured, Chris aides these strangers, entwining his future with theirs.

Now that the vampires know the hunters are here, and that Chris and his friends have helped them, the group is in more danger than ever before. Lucas is torn between protecting his new family from the vampires, and protecting them from these seemingly inhuman beings who say they are there to help.

After all, what beings could be so powerful as to scare a vampire?

Available in paperback through your local book dealer or Createspace https://www.createspace.com/4112865

Available in e-book through Smashwords

https://www.smashwords.com/books/view/270492

Angels & Warriors: The Awakening

by Dawn Tevy

In the novel, 'Angels & Warriors, The Awakening,' author Dawn Tevy introduces you to characters that are funny, loving, and artfully scheming... Our heroin, Lady Tynae, finds herself in a precarious situation when she is hunted down by those she most trusts. In a single heartbeat her fairly simple life becomes incredibly complicated. Finding herself in a new world full of magic, dragons, and an old friend, Tynae soon discovers nothing in her life was ever as it appeared. The vivid scenes and descriptive dialogue will transport you to another place. This spectacular fantasy world is set in a time and land that has slowly faded into the haziness of legend and lore. Between discovering her new world and falling in love, Tynae must uncover what lies at her very core. She is accomplished with swords, an expert marksman, and she even knows how to bring a full grown man to his knees...but is she the 'Chosen One'?

Available in paperback and E-book from Amazon

http://www.amazon.com/books/dp/0615602002